NOTHING COMES BACK

NOTHING COMES BACK

Stories

SUSAN E. LLOY

|N₁|O₂|N₁

CANADA

*Publisher's note: This book is a work of fiction. Names, characters, places and
incidents are either the product of the author's imagination or are used
fictitiously, and any resemblance to actual persons living or dead
is entirely coincidental.*

Library and Archives Canada Cataloguing in Publication

Title: Nothing comes back : stories / Susan E. Lloy.

Names: Lloy, Susan E., 1957- author.

Identifiers: Canadiana (print) 20220482004 | Canadiana (ebook) 20220482020 |
ISBN 9781989689486 (softcover) | ISBN 9781989689523 (EPUB)

Classification: LCC PS8623.L678 N68 2023 | DDC C813/.6—dc23

Printed and bound in Canada on 100% recycled paper.

Now Or Never Publishing
901, 163 Street
Surrey, British Columbia
Canada V4A 9T8

nonpublishing.com
Fighting Words.

We gratefully acknowledge the support of the Canada Council for the Arts
and the British Columbia Arts Council for our publishing program.

Forever, Nicolas

Contents

Contents

Nothing Comes Back

Sybil has never been good at letting go. Not her loved ones, not a pair of old shoes, not even a jacket she hasn't worn in twenty years. So, when she arrived at her new abode, she managed to drag loads of stuff that she knew she would never use and was left with the task of not knowing what to do with or where to store all of it. It is a small apartment and space will be problematic. Now that she is retired and free, she feels deflated and confined.

She had never been good at planning her life and fell into a dead-end job with a paltry salary in her early forties after travelling and changing countless meaningless positions. Retirement still seemed a long ways off. Yet, here she is, with scant money coming in from her pension and little savings. Dreams of travel and escape are far out of reach. As she stands with an unpacked moving box at her feet she thinks to herself, *Fuck… this is what it's all come down to.*

She has returned to her place of birth following forty-five years away and finds it hard to believe that she is actually here. Growing up she longed to escape this place, but here she is living in a section of the city she always despised. There was no other choice. This corner of her pocket-sized world is the most afford-able, but neighbours are in close proximity, balconies touch each other like shoulders watching a parade.

When she looks at her contemporaries she still feels young, though today, catching a glimpse of her reflection in the harsh afternoon light she realizes she is getting on. She has one child, a daughter whom she rarely sees. Antonia, her spawn, has no intention of leaving the big city for a smaller one and isn't plan-ning a visit to her mother any time soon. They have always had a strained relationship. Not for any particular reason. They are like two opposite forces that repel instead of attract.

Antonia is an artist. A painter, who struggles and refuses to give up her dreams of becoming *one of them*. She believes she has it, even when gallery after gallery refuses to give her a show. Antonia is striking with an unusual red birthmark on the left side of her face shaped like a seahorse. Her mother always insisted it was a beauty mark declaring it made her special. But, Antonia never bought into it and the mistrust and difficulties began right there.

Sybil has never been what one would label joyful. Not as a child, not as a youth and not now in later life. Sure there had been good times, especially when she was tripping in the spring of early womanhood. Now everything seems flat. Expired. Occasionally, when she hears an old loved tune she will perk up. Dance about, remembering a time when things felt possible, yet when the song is finished she is left alone in the silence. A vacuum.

She doesn't know how her world became this inconsequential. It is down to less than a handful of people. Because of this she has developed an unhealthy addiction to rummaging the Internet, searching out former lovers, classmates and foes.

Sybil lets out a sigh as she examines the unpacked boxes. She has an abundance of photographs. Some of these photos haven't been looked at in years and she can't remember some of the people's names that are in them, but they remind her of a livelier time and this is why she keeps them. However, looking at them now she imagines if she dropped dead this very instant there would be so many things for Antonia to go through. She expels the thought from her mind.

The walls are thin here and she can hear the neighbours' televisions and stereos. The one upstairs is a stomper and she can tell whomever it is wears shoes. She will have to have a word, explaining that she suffers from misophonia and could they not wear them inside. Sybil knows she will hate it here. She stands on her compact balcony listening to a brood of gulls call across the grey, drizzly sky.

One box contains a bundle of cards. Love letters from her ex—Antonia's father. He is long gone, yet Sybil thinks Antonia will find solace in the words and perceive that she was created within a time of affection. Antonia was young when her father left. It's part of her bitterness. Her dubiosity.

Sybil unwraps one of Antonia's paintings. She is a figurative painter. It's a self-portrait with a distorted face somewhat in the vein of Francis Bacon, her idol. It is disturbing to think that Antonia thinks of herself like this, but Sybil hangs it in a prominent spot with a wall all to itself. Her breathing is laboured as she examines it.

Life has become small. Sybil isn't on any social media sites such as Facebook. She has access though, from a time when Antonia used her computer. It has become an unproductive habit. Looking for old lovers and people she has long lost contact with. Examining their lives, and partners. New kitchens, trips and what seem all the pleasantries of life. Sybil had let friends drop from her life. It seems like her life had been put on hold while others had moved on. If she reached out a reply would come, still it was her that had to do all the reaching. All those old friends in foreign lands had long forgotten her. Or had intentionally ignored her. It was if all the cozy worlds she once was part of had imploded and she was left with only a chill travelling her spine. Correspondence became painful, with the usual—*same ol'* at the end of every email.

She painfully organizes the apartment; however another purge will be necessary. A neighbour's television bellows through the wall. As she lets out a long sigh, she ponders packing the whole place up and heading to the country. Somewhere rural. Close to the sea. An old magazine lies on the coffee table with a double-spread of the Grand Canyon displaying all of its glory. The reds and rusts are warm and inviting and seem to say, *What are you waiting for?*

She doesn't have money socked away for extensive travels, but a little for one special trip. Sybil had always wanted to visit the Grand Canyon and areas beyond. The desert. It was always near, especially when there was some commercial or film with its uplifted Proterozoic and Paleozoic strata and vividly-hued landscapes. Rivers, rapids, valleys with canyons and walls built of ancient rock. How breathtaking and humbling it must feel to stand within.

She has done her homework and knows it is a relatively short drive through from Vegas. Utah would be next heading to Zion National Park. She extends the invitation to Antonia to tag along, but her daughter declines insisting that she is immersed in a new series of works. It hurts Sybil. This tension between them runs like a fierce river. Unflinching and constant.

For the most part her clothes remain unpacked with fabrics hanging over opened boxes. She still holds on to items that are too small or too young. Nevertheless, she has kept them for her own unsound reasons, a trove of clutter and useless accumulation. She snatches up a flimsy top for the warm weather. Who knows? Maybe she'll meet someone.

Her flight is the following week. She plans to stay one night in Vegas and make an early start the following morning. The itinerary is well coordinated and would usually take two and a half hours to reach Springdale in Utah, but she plans to stretch it out taking time for rest stops and scenic vistas. When she reaches her destination for the day, she'll stay a night in Springdale and hike the following day to Weeping Rock in Zion National Park.

Sybil has done a little research and there is something about Weeping Rock that speaks to her. A kindred spirit, so she thinks. It isn't merely the name, but also the photographs she has examined of the place, where the water continually seeps at the junction of two strata creating an arena of ferns, moss and wildflowers. An oasis on the side of a ridge. She imagines herself being able to breathe freely there. Free of confinement and neighbourly clamor.

Weeping Rock evokes a consciousness and awakens a part of her being that has been shut down. She feels that she needs a good cry. A release. And imagines she will get it there for the rock is forever wailing, as if its heart has been broken into a million bits.

Her flight is the following day. Most of the packing has been done save for a few boxes. She had put up shelves and arranged books. Hung favourite pieces on walls. It has begun to feel more like her, yet she doesn't see herself here. It's as if she watches herself from a different sphere. As if she was a character in some film.

The heat assaults her as she hits Las Vegas. She has a place on the strip for one night at Planet Hollywood Resort & Casino and heads directly to her suite via the hotel-airport shuttle. It is midafternoon and the sun hangs high in the sky, but there is plenty of time to explore the strip, have dinner and play a few slot machines before retiring. Her road trip will commence after breakfast the following day.

It is the first time in her life to take in a casino. She has fifty dollars to play with. Not a penny more. The minute she sits down she becomes annoyed. There is noise everywhere. From boisterous loud drunks to screaming bachelorettes, bells ring and lights blink. It's all a bit too much. In spite of the bedlam she thinks, *What the hell, I might as well give it a go*. And go it does, on the second try. Sybil pulls the lever and PANG, out comes a ticket with a barcode. I won!

Everyone claps and shouts. Some look on with disdain. *Why not me?* Sybil turns in her ticket for a twenty-four thousand dollar cheque. She can't believe her luck. Not bad for a five dollar investment. She treats herself to a good meal at the casino restaurant and heads back to her room to tuck in for an early night.

She has rented a Volkswagen Bug Convertible for the trip. She wants the wind in her hair and sun on her face. All of her senses opened for unfamiliar awakenings. The car is being dropped off at the hotel's entrance. It is a shiny dark bronze metallic. It will mirror the colours of the canyon. She has purchased supplies for the expedition such as water, sandwiches and a bottle of good wine.

Edwin Smith lives in Wasatch County, Utah, on a ranch not far from Salt Lake City. Edwin prides himself on being a direct descendant of Joseph Smith, the forefather of the Polygamy movement. He is not a genetic heir, but offspring of one of his five adopted children, although proclaim has been impossible to prove. Edwin grew up in the faith. As far as he can remember his kin had practiced plural marriage, as does he with his eleven wives, twenty-three children and five grandchildren.

Edwin is in his early sixties and still possesses a good physique, takes pride in his appearance and is a member of the Utah Film Industry. He still works as a grip on films now and again. He bought this ranch in the early eighties. By that time he had long given up the notion that the more the merrier bought one a ticket to a special spot in the celestial kingdom. No, by that time he simply enjoyed the idea that plural marriage was a good thing. Made a more interesting, spicier life for a man.

Most of his wives were sealed by traditional practice, although there had been no prophet involved. Two of his ladies came from the film industry for Edwin was quite the catch in his youth. The others were locals and an old school sweetheart and had been chosen at a time when he held close to the thought that more kin were the best route to heaven. Through time the group had adjusted to these changes and the departures from the rigid rules of the church, which they had been accustomed to.

Locals frowned upon them and called them the 'Smithsters' and thought of them more like a cult than an offshoot of the Mormon faith, who are their neighbours in all directions. Initially, they tried to make a go of it by subsistence farming. Producing cheese, baking their famous Smithster pies, but ranching is a tough trade and because most of the clan had film expertise, they sought out a different direction of income— producing soft porn.

As righteous as folks like to think of themselves around here and beyond, sometimes they need extra flavor added to the mix. Things become rigid and boring. Edwin found a niche in this market and made a tidy living from their film production company. Edwin and his two wives who sprung from film work had educated the others in distribution and marketing. Some were designated to costume design, while others dealt with the children and managed mealtimes and the overall daily goings on about the ranch.

Mostly all of them acted in the films in some capacity, or they subcontracted parts out advertising in open casting calls for adult films or by word of mouth.

Their porn is subtle: naked women bailing hay, selling baked goods at a country fair, frolicking in a haystack, the local sheriff putting on the cuffs.

It draws a special sort of clientele. Country folk and farmers. People seeking a refuge from the Bible Belt dogma, which is the norm in this belief-filled land.

Sybil enjoys her road trip and the stunning panoramas along her route, but now she is in Zion National Park and plans to lunch in Springfield, then hike the Weeping Rock trailhead. There are a multitude of places to eat along the Zion Park Blvd, but she settles in at The Spotted Dog Café and orders a hearty meal of roast beef, mashed potatoes, grilled vegetables and coffee. She figures she will need it for the trail ahead.

Before she leaves, she writes a postcard to Antonia. Sybil likes this lost world of card sending. Now everything is encased within a phone. She imagines Antonia caressing the image with her paint-stained fingers and lovingly placing it a special spot, thinking to herself, *I should have gone on that trip*. But truth be told, Antonia could care less.

Sybil enters the trail and begins her ascent. Edwin has finished a shoot. He is currently working on a series where multiples of sophisticated and often erotic robots act out individuals' fantasies in a futuristic theme park. The location is not far from Weeping Rock and is a lovely spot that Edwin finds himself repeatedly drawn to again and again. Sybil has chosen it too, though she is enticed by unknown reasons. They are like two bodies that submit to the force of attraction like sun and earth, earth and moon.

Sybil reaches Weeping Rock and rests her bones on a bench overlooking a carved out valley. The weeping water cascades over hanging gardens, which are moist with lush vegetation. The sounds are gentle and the smells rich. There are few visitors today and Sybil is content. She is alone save for one or two strays who stroll by every twenty minutes or so.

As she sits, she goes over her life. Antonia is her only kin. She wishes her late sister were next to her. Her ashes lie on a bookshelf in her new apartment. They say a loved one's remains are a mix of many cremations. She hopes her sister is mixed with fun folk. Sybil watches the water and contemplates: *will this be her last trip? Will Antonia get her big break? Will their relationship ever heal? Will she ever get laid again?* It's been over two decades since she has been intimate. It feels like a lost world, something intangible, as if trying to reconstruct a dream after awaking.

Edwin arrives soon after his wrap. He has always liked this spot and remembers coming here as a child with his sister-moms, brothers and sisters. They would have picnics and look out over the land believing that they had arrived in heaven, or at the very least, were nearly there. What could be more beautiful than this carved-out landscape? Though truthfully he just wants to get away from all of the hullabaloo at the ranch. With the constant screaming of the youngsters and whose night it would be amongst the wives. The rooster that is eternally argued over.

He sits on an opposite side of the look-out and takes in all of its beauty, letting out a deep breath after reaching this elevation. There is only himself and Sybil who sit staring out at the weeping water at this precise moment. Edwin remembers running around here with his siblings. Youth was a happy time. There was always someone to play with, make a fort or battle off invisible enemies between chores. He has lost touch with most of his brothers and sisters, as they do not approve of the porn.

"Certainly is a pretty spot, don't you think?"

"Yes. There's no denying that."

"Mind if I park next to you?"

Edwin places himself on the bench next to Sybil. She is nervous. It feels like at least five incarnations ago since a man has flirted with her.

"I'm Edwin."

"Sybil."

"Well, nice to meet you, Sybil."

Edwin smiles and Sybil notices his handsome windblown face, his good teeth and full head of unruly grey hair, which blows this way and that. He is fit, without a paunch, and she is uneasy feeling a hot flash coming on. She starts fanning herself with her empty lunch bag.

"Are you a tourist or from around these parts?"

"A tourist. Your northern neighbour to be exact. Canada."

"Oh, where there?"

"I left Montreal recently and have resettled in Nova Scotia, which I left just short of a half a century ago. Man! Can't believe I just said that. How did we get this far?"

"How do you find returning to your ol' homestead after such a long time away?"

"It's quite strange. I'm not at all sure I've made the right decision."

"Well... I'm from this wonderful land. Would you care to visit some other areas of interest?"

"I'm not sure about that. I have a fixed itinerary and my rental car is due back at a specified time."

"Hey, don't dwell on simple details. You can save yourself some cash, plus visit some places you hadn't thought of. Return your car at the nearest drop-off. I've got some time off work. I work in the film industry and just finished a week's worth of shoots. What do you say?"

Sybil's mind is racing. Who is this guy? He could very well be a serial killer, rapist or just a mere kook. Still, there is something in the tone of his voice and the spaces between his words that makes her trust him.

The rental is dropped off in Springfield and they embark on a tour of Bryce Canyon and Capital Reef. Moab. The trip takes just over three days. They hunt for fossils and love the silence amidst the layered rock. Edwin is charming and affectionate. His touch warms her like a fire on a winter's eve. All those years she remained celibate… sometimes even the massage from the hairdresser's assistant would fill her being with uneasiness. A mere brush to the body that had been without intimate contact stirred the emptiness inside her.

On their second evening, they slept together. Sybil had been nervous and restrained, but following a couple bottles of good wine, she relaxed and melted into him. However, she is no spring chicken and, though her joints are not as limber as they once were and personal dexterity has become more challenging, she's pleased that she didn't end up in a full body cast with one leg supported by traction, which both surprised and relieved her. On the third evening Edwin proposed. Sybil was about to accept, yet before she can let the word escape from her lips he covers her mouth softly with his forefinger.

"Sybil. I must disclose something before you reply. I'm a polygamist. I have eleven other wives and, if you agree, you shall be the twelfth. We are not fundamentalists. I grew up in that strict world, but our family isn't based on restrictions. Our values are communal. Shared work ethic regarding child rearing and household tasks, friendship and love."

Sybil's thoughts are whizzing. *What is this? Who is this? What have I got myself into? He could be a proper psycho. Well, hold your horses. We had a three day-fling. We're not exactly involved…*

"Before you make a decision, why not come to our ranch for a visit? Meet the family, have a meal. Try a few days."

Sybil agrees, though she isn't sure why. The whole arrangement sounds wildly weird. Nevertheless, she calls Antonia to announce her new plans. She'd met a guy and will prolong her stay a little while. Antonia listens without offering advice or warning or even 'have a good time'.

"Uh-huh. OK. 'Til later."

Sybil sits silent for the ride as they travel to the foothills of the Wasatch Mountain Range. Edwin sings a song and reassuringly rubs her knee. It is a beautiful spread hosting a large main house with smaller homes side by side and what appears to be a huge garage behind. There are goats, chickens, pigs and cows. Horses lazily graze in another pasture. Three barns sit in the distance. As they approach, children run towards the truck laughing and waving eager to greet, Edwin their keeper.

Edwin had telephoned ahead to alert his first wife of his intentions. She was to go down the line informing the other ten wives of a possible twelfth. One by one the women approached, all of varied ages. The youngest three probably in their twenties or early thirties. Sybil is surprised to see that they all look normal. No strange hairdos or pioneer type conservative attire. They wear jeans, T-shirts and Converses. A few with cool summer dresses.

The first wife, Meryl, who is around the same age as herself, comes towards her holding out her hand and welcoming her with a big, toothy smile.

"Hello, Sybil. Nice to have you here."

The others saunter over to make her acquaintance. Sybil makes eye contact immediately forgetting each of their names. Too many, too fast.

"We've prepared a tasty meal."

Sybil is given a tour of the main house, which is clean and simply decorated. Photographs grace the walls showcasing the generations of multiple kin, some display 19th century garb and women sporting weird pompadour hairdos. They head out to the back of the house where a handcrafted wooden table roughly thirty feet long is situated with a similar sized table for the children off to the side. The meal is delicious and the atmosphere amicable, although from time to time Sybil catches the leer of a jealous wife sizing her up. Calculating competition.

After three days at the ranch Sybil accepts Edwin's proposal. She likes the idea of company, not being on her own. Although she could only retrieve a tiny hint of the other wives feelings towards her, she imagines they will warm up to her. Sybil FaceTimes with Antonia and invites her to the wedding, but Antonia declines saying, "Mom! Are you out of your mind?"

They are sealed in an open garden with Edwin leading the ceremony. Not that he holds true in his heart these sacraments. No, he likes the idea of another lady added to the pot. He has not expressed this to Sybil, but her savings and pension must be added to the family purse. While she is having a bath following their two-day honeymoon, Edwin transfers her savings to his bank account. Now that she is married, he contacts her bank informing them all funds and investments must be e-transferred to their joint account. All of her passwords and personal information are easy to find; she doesn't have the best security money-transfer apps on her iPhone—bank passwords, investments and pension access are easily accessible. Security questions are ready to submit. He had taken a photo of her signature when she returned the rental car. All he had to do was Login, send a false, forged photo of the marriage license and Bob's your uncle!

It took Sybil some time before she noticed that something was amiss. She discovered this when attempting to draw cash from her account after she was handed her measly allowance by Meryl. She contacted her bank immediately, but they assured her that no fraud had taken place. Her husband, Edwin Smith, had authorized the transfers to their new joint account. After all, her status had changed. She was no longer single. Without taking further action, Sybil decides to sit on it for a bit, but tells the bank this is not the last of it. Edwin is now far from her heart. How could he do this without consulting her first?

Before she gets to confront him on the matter, Edwin is off on a film shoot. He will be gone for a few weeks. Sybil is added to the work schedule.

In the days prior to his departure, Sybil was already bounced down on the romance docket. The younger wives given preference. The older wives, including herself, tabbed further down for sleepovers.

Sybil had been allotted a room in the main house. There were ten bedrooms in this roost. It was a bright square room flooded with natural light. When she was given work duties in the house, such as dusting and vacuuming and whenever she was alone in the house, she explored. She examined each and every bedroom. Checked out the attire in each closet. For example, which wife had a better clothes collection and who had better shoes. She formed a hierarchy blueprint of this plural marriage.

One particularly warm, cloudless day Sybil heard a commotion. There was a small minibus of young, fit ladies filling the backyard area of the main house. She was curious if these fresh bits of flesh would be added to the fuse. She wandered over to the yard watching the ladies enter the huge outbuilding two by two. Until now Sybil had not been invited to this part of the ranch, but hey… wasn't she one of them? At least for now.

The space is open and grandiose. The minute she entered she realizes it's a film set. There are lighting kits and booms, video cameras and sets partially built or complete. She spots Meryl and a few of the other wives sitting inspecting the ladies from the minibus. They are instructed to remove their clothing and strut their stuff. Sybil can't quite grasp the meaning of it all and slowly walks closer for a peek.

"Sybil, come here. So what do you think?"

"Of what exactly?"

"These ladies, what else?"

"Well, they're lovely. But what are they doing here?"

"Didn't Edwin tell you about our production compay? Peek A Boo Films."

"No. Actually he did not."

"Well, we do pretty well with it. We produce soft-core pornography."

"Oh, do you now?"

"The farm can't run on its own steam, so we started this about fifteen years ago and it brings in quite a tidy sum."

Sybil takes it all in all the while fuming at Edwin's lack of disclosure. First it was her bank accounts and now this. She doesn't have any moral hang-ups on the subject. Hell, she even danced in an erotic club to pay her way through university once upon a time. Yet, how many more secrets are buried on this land?

Nearly one month has passed since she had set foot on the ranch. After the initial honeymoon, she felt familiar naggings and doubts nipping at her ankles. She felt like an outsider amongst the other wives. Fuck, even the children paid her no mind and she was pissed at being left alone following Edwin's quick departure. Her savings and casino winnings had been swept away in what seemed a microsecond and if her money was simmering in the family pot she was barely getting a whiff of it.

She had telephoned and texted Antonia countless times, but typically, Antonia didn't respond. Antonia had come into some luck. She was to have her own show at one of the city's big galleries. She had immersed herself in her work preparing multiple large pieces for the exhibition that would open in one week.

She had noticed her mother's messages, but didn't want to be distracted by some lament that she expected was to come, for some of Sybil's texts were dramatic and crazed. Antonia had been working on a portrait. It is her homage to Sybil. It is a large piece taking one wall of the gallery.

Sybil is isolated on a flat background with a distorted face and open mouth suggesting a scream. The face is somewhat grotesque and her hair is swept up over her forehead in an exaggerated pompadour. She sports a prairie dress that hangs to her feet. The painting is strange and alarming, with dark pigments layering the canvas. Yet, it demands the viewer to stare. It evokes feelings of confinement and withdrawal. The portrait sells on opening night to a prominent collector. Antonia sends a photo to her mother with a red circle next to the title, which simply reads—Sybil.

Synthesis of a Dream

The day is upon him and one that he's dreading—retirement. It isn't that he's worried about what to do. No. No. It's fusion. His wife, Tess, had been an interior designer and had retired one year earlier. He dealt with numbers and finance and between them they have acquired quite the tidy sum. The two of them are to sail off into the sunset. Literally. They plan to buy a sailboat and do just that.

Tess is a thoughtful wife. She fusses. Making sure his clothes are always ready to go, fresh from the cleaners. Dinners arranged as if professionally catered. The house and atmosphere are a delight to the eye. In his youth he had appreciated her attention to detail, not only for the tactile, but also for himself.

He loved her passionately when they were young, yet now they have settled into a life based on habit and old dreams. Tess adores him as much as she did the moment they met, but he has drifted away. She never stops to catch her breath, droning on about how they will spend every waking minute together. Buying groceries, taking walks. Wining and dining. Seeing the world as one. The mere thought of them cooped up on a boat creates a tightness in his chest and makes his skin crawl. *How has he become this man?*

They are a childless couple. Believing it their moral duty not to add more beings to this fucked-up world. Throughout their lives they did charitable work when time permitted. Time is theirs now. They had always sailed. Owning a small sloop at their summer home. In later years, they studied navigation, learning to manage larger boats, venturing into deeper waters. The idea of sailing the world had always been a mutual aspiration.

They had long sold their summer getaway and more recently their home. They had been eyeing boats for six months and had settled on an eleven year-old Amel with a fiberglass hull presently docked in Nice, France. It is fifty-six feet long, modern and elegant. It has been well maintained with three cabins and is praised for its performance and safety. It came in just under six hundred thousand American dollars. The new Amel models go for well over two million Euros. Slightly out of their range.

A pied-à-terre was purchased in the hip part of downtown. A place to rest their sea legs on sailing breaks. Tess had kept all of her favourite finds. *Oh, Boris, shall we take this along?* Boris just shrugs and feels like he's being propelled like a paper catboat in a city pond. Why doesn't he just step up and say, '*I don't want any of this*', is way beyond him. He's become a shadow of his former self. Tess is the doer. Boris lets her have that role and she is doing and arranging and pushing him along as he has always permitted. *Can he about-face now?*

He assumes it's a sort of depression. The end of an era. The finish line, so to speak. He does not feel lucky now that he's free of work stress or that the bank account is flush. He just envisions sentences being answered, Tess's appetite for intimacy that is never quenched, her relentless retells and high-pitched laugh.

They are young to retire, both in their mid-fifties. Tess still looks good. She never went for the nips and tucks or fillers, though the money was there if she had wanted to. She is existentially sound. Nevertheless, Boris finds it hard to meet her sexual demands. In recent years he has become uninterested, only aroused by watching porn, any other woman. Hey, he even had an escort or two. He does feel guilty, though. Tess doesn't deserve his deceit. He hides it in his pocket like a dirty image from a magazine.

They fly to Nice. Their boat, which is christened Tango, is docked at the Port Lympia of Nice. A hotel near the beach is booked for a week until their sailboat is ready to leave its comfy mooring. The interior is composed of exotic woods, with mahogany being the primary hardwood. There is a large dining room table with comfortable cushioned white seating. In fact, all of the furniture under deck is white. Tess has already ordered a brightly coloured Sunbrella fabric for the upper deck and lower cabins. She wants to add her personal touch.

The 56' ketch-rigged sailboat has one covered helm station and three individual cabins under the deck. The galley has stainless steel appliances with a propane stove and oven, microwave. The captain's cabin, which is near the bow, hosts a king size bed with overhead shelving and ample storage. One sleeper cabin is near the stern with a queen size bed and the other is off the main living quarters with two built-in bunk beds.

Tess runs around town collecting this and that: a treasured lamp, a favourite dish, textiles—both primitive and modern. The boat will be as eclectic as their former home. Boris sits these sessions out and Tess doesn't pressure him. He enjoys relaxing on their hotel balcony, sipping cocktails and eyeing women strolling the boardwalk. The small city sprawls below its pastel-hued glory. Lean shutters grace the many-windowed buildings and tidy boats moored at their docks shimmer in the harbour's reflective calm.

Often he goes to the beach examining topless ladies bronzing in the sunlit sand. Tess would never go for nude public bathing. She has a prudish side to her that continues to annoy him even after all these years of marriage. In two days their friends, Beau and Maryann, will join them. They are recent retirees and are excited to be the first invited guests to set sail.

Tess is happy with the boat. She has made it her own. Boris has always appreciated her good taste, letting her do what she wants in every aspect of their thirty-five years of cohabitation. They will stay in Nice for a few days escorting their guests around its quaint shops and cafés. They meet Beau and Maryann at the airport refreshed from first-class pampering.

"Boris! Tess! How lovely to see you again."

They kiss each other on each cheek. Even Boris joins in this French greeting.

"How was your flight?"

"Great. We were served fantastic food, champagne and we had the pods, you know. After a few we both fell dead asleep until just before landing."

"Nice. First we'll get you settled. Your suite is on the same floor as ours. Take your time. Get rejuvenated and text us when you're ready to go."

They spend the next three days enjoying the sights, swimming at the beach, inspecting the sailboat, drinking wine and buying provisions for the voyage.

Beau inquires how life is for Boris since his retirement, but Boris shrugs his questions off and seems unenthused about his present arrangements. Tess, on the other hand, is giddy. Enveloped with fervor about recent design changes to the boat, not having anyone to answer to, free from deadlines, and most of all—having Boris all to herself.

Beau and Maryann had often sailed with Boris and Tess at their summer home. They seemed like good sailors, however their sailboat had been a different beast. A small boat. Tango moors at the dock gleaming in the hot afternoon sun, defiant and headstrong. This sailboat requires a hands-on crew, and even though the waters of the Mediterranean are beautiful beyond description, the sea is more than three miles deep in spots and strong winds can be unpredictable blowing from the land to the centre of the sea.

These winds have names. One originates from the Sahara, another from southern France, and then there are the winds from Croatia, Greece and Turkey. The differences between land and sea also create localized breezes that are northern in the morning, variable at midday and strong southerly in the afternoon, which makes it challenging for even the most experienced sailors.

Added to the mix is a strong surface current, especially in summer, caused by the sea's surface water evaporating faster than the rivers can replenish it. All of these facts gnaw at Maryann's mind causing her to observe Boris' and Tess' movements on the boat with intense interest and concern.

The first day of the trip Maryann is more at ease, as the agenda had been kept secret. A surprise. They will hang close to shore sailing from Nice to Antibes, Cannes, Saint-Tropez, Toulon and finally ending up in Marseille where Beau and Maryann will fly back home. The sun is high and the sea calm as they leave the sheltered harbour. They feel assured as the ketch slips out into open water and relieved that land is always within eyeshot. Boris and Tess appear confident and the wind is suitable for stable sailing.

Boris asks Beau to take the helm and steer while he and Tess position the sails. Occasionally, they ask Maryann to assist with jibing and tacking.

"Watch your head, Maryann!"

It proves to be quite exhilarating. They dock at Port Vauban and take in the sights while scouting out a restaurant in the small town. They are all a little tired from the sea air. The aperitifs and wine kick in quickly. Tess melts into Boris at the table, but Boris shrinks away and appears annoyed.

"Come on, Tess. Christ, we've been together non-stop. Give me a break."

Maryann and Beau remain silent while Maryann reaches for Tess' knee under the table and rubs it reassuringly. Beau quizzes Boris about investments and they settle in to a relatively silent dinner at Taverne Saint-Jacques.

Following a delicious dinner and much wine, they slowly saunter the quiet streets back towards the port. There isn't a lot of jabber during the return trip and, upon arrival at the boat, each couple heads to their respective quarters to retire for the night.

Next morning Tess is the first up and Maryann soon follows. They let their men snooze into the morning and prepare freshly squeezed orange juice, scrambled eggs and bacon. Toast and coffee.

"Tess, how did you sleep? How are you feeling?"

"Oh fine. Boris had one of his moods. There seems to be more of them lately. Maybe retirement isn't what he expected."

"Well, you're both pretty damn fortunate. Lots of mullah and a life many would kill for. Do you think that's all it is?"

"I don't know. Boris has never been what one would call a talker. After all these years, half the time I have no clue what goes on in that head of his."

Just as the espresso pot starts to hiss two groggy men enter the galley smiling at the generously set table. They sit down to breakfast and discuss the itinerary for the following days. Boris tries to be his old self, but his gloomy mood still lingers on like a damp, drizzly afternoon. Tess ignores the darkened atmosphere and jumps into her rose-coloured demeanour while the men head to deck. Maryann and Tess clean up and prepare a lunch of crab salad, croissants and various cheeses for the sail to Cannes. Rosé and beer are chilling in the fridge and the sun gleams through the cabin's windows. Once again they are blessed by clear skies and a soft wind agreeable for sailing. Maryann thinks about discussing Boris with Tess, but reconsiders and heads up to the deck to join the men.

Boris belts out instructions to Beau and they are on their way. It isn't a long sail and before arriving at Cannes they anchor to lunch and swim. The sea is warm and the blue sky and water seems to call all on deck.

"Tess. How does Boris seem to you? He's a little out of sorts. I never remember him being grumpy and short to vex. Is everything all right with you two?"

"Yeah, for the most part. I think retirement is proving a harder adjustment than he anticipated. He's not the sort with a lot of projects on the go and he sees the future as a long, troubled breath. I thought this boat would be the answer to his angst, but it doesn't seem to be doing the trick."

Because of his consistent cheerlessness, Tess begins to see him in a different light. Is this what her future will be, constantly manoeuvring around his shifting disposition? As she watches him dive off the deck into the deep water she fleetingly thinks, *I hope the hell he stays down there.*

Their days prove to be concurrently strained and pleasant. Maryann and Tess separate from the men to walk the Boulevard de la Croisette, shopping and taking in the sights. Boris and Beau decide to roam the old town away from the glitz heading to Suquet to lunch amidst its sloping, cobbled walkways. Café upon restaurant lining the cozy alleys. They choose a quaint, intimate corner and immediately order wine while soaking up the local atmosphere. Each lost in thought.

"What's up, Boris? Everything all right?"

"Yeah, for the most part. I mean what's not to like about this place?"

"True, but I'm referring to you and Tess. We've noticed a tension that was never there before."

"Well… you know I didn't expect it to be like this."

"Like what?"

"Hog-tied on a boat with Tess 24/7. You see work created separation, now it's too much. I can't take it. Maybe I'm purely in metamorphosis mode, but if this is how it will be for the rest of my days… FUCK, is just about all I can say."

"Boris, man, you know you're charmed, right? You have money. Tess is a kind woman and she still looks great. What were you expecting at this juncture?"

"That's just it. I don't know anymore."

As they sit passing away the hours, Boris thinks it would be nice to exist in a parallel world free of doubt, frustration and temptation.

They continue to drink in the warm afternoon, becoming lazy after consuming a large seafood lunch and return to the boat to relax and nap. Maybe catch a fish for fun. Maryann and Tess arrive a few hours later laden with purses, dresses and shoes.

The following days imitate the previous—swimming, short sailing trips, walks around old towns and long lingering dinners. It seems like the world's problems are in an alternate universe. The sunshine prevents any previously murky thoughts from penetrating like fully armoured warriors. By the time they arrive in Marseille they all need to rest their sea legs. A good hotel is chosen for the last two days before Maryann and Beau head home. They continue to meet for meals and take in the sights. Beau and Tess have been making an effort, yet on their last evening together the strain between them bursts like a flash flood.

In between courses at a high-end restaurant they discuss their next voyage, a crossing from Marseille to Carcassonne, on to Barcelona, Malaga, through Gibraltar to Cadiz and finally Lisbon. The argument erupts about whether the trip should be spread over several weeks or should be expedited. They fight over possible port stops, hours of sailing per day, whether to sail through the night or dock for the evening. Boris wants to get going as soon as possible, but Tess wants to enjoy the safety of a friendly harbour when daylight hours have long settled in for nightfall.

Their voices become elevated and the waiter paces nervously around the table. Patrons raise their eyebrows at the confrontation. Words can be heard close to them.

"Des Anglais, merde!"

"Wow. Boris, Tess, is this necessary?"

"This is our shit, Beau."

"Come on, man. This is our last evening together. Is it going to end like this?"

"You're right. Sorry. So, sorry. Let's get back on track."

Following the feud, things seem to settle down. Maryann and Beau make immediate eye contact when Tess gets up to visit the ladies' room and Boris heads outside to smoke a cigar.

"I just can't imagine how the rest of their trip is going to go. It's apparent there is a lot of trouble in them waters. Truthfully, I'm glad to go home. This is getting all too warring. I feel bad for Tess, though. I mean you can see she's trying, but Boris, he's becoming more difficult each day."

Boris is upset with himself, nevertheless he can't put back what's no longer there. Even the idea of growing old together and familiar creature comforts of a long friendship grate on his nerves. He is consumed with dark awareness as he smokes, watching the smoke drift up towards the night sky.

There isn't much to say following farewells at the airport.

"Well, Tess. It's just you and me now."

Tess smiles at Boris and gently caresses his arm as they head back to the hotel. Two days are allotted for gathering supplies for the next leg of travel. The long range weather forecast is optimistic, yet there is a heaviness in the air, which trumps all else. They dine in Marseille before leaving early the next morning. Uneasiness and words are stuck as if flies to a sticky paper. They wish to express what is building between them, but they chew their food in silence avoiding eye contact and distracting themselves with fine wine.

Tango leaves her moor and proudly heads to open water. The sea is choppy and the sun struggles to be seen. The water is dark as they make their way out to sea. It will be a nine-hour sail from Marseille to Barcelona. The forecast is for unsettled weather with a dense fog. There could be thunderstorms brewing and the wind has picked up making it necessary for all hands on deck.

They had argued about setting out in a system where winds might prove sharp and violent. All of their skills could be tested. Tess had wanted to stay put in a well-sheltered harbour, but Boris was eager to get going and test Tango in conditions where she would have to perform like a well-behaved lady. He wants to know that their training has proven beneficial. Boris protests that, "We just can't sit pretty in a safe haven all the time. Let's get out there and test what we've got. It will increase our confidence." Yet, Tess is pissed at him and nervous as they head out. Land has become invisible.

The wind comes at them with force and anger. Tess hears Boris shouting.

"We're tipping! We have to reef the main! Ease the boom, Tess! We have to right her!"

She runs to follow his instructions, but hesitates for a moment, turning an image she saw on his cellphone over and over in her head. She had found text messages from a young woman in Nice with blatant sexual acquaintance and nude photos, hints that only an intimate could know. So, instead of taking up the topping lift she lets it slacken and the boom swings out of control, striking Boris with a direct hit. She's not sure if her hesitation was intentional.

She quickly hoists the main and tightens the sails, trimming the mainsheet to get Tango under control by pointing into the wind. She steers her towards the coast and calls a Mayday on the radio. She throws a couple of life jackets over the side, though too distant for Boris to reach. As she approaches, the fog lifts and land is within sight. She feels ethereal as she sits at the helm assured that the boat has submitted to her.

LINGERIE

He has been watching her for some time. She comes to do laundry once a week and always offers up a half smile, acknowledging him, but never engaging in conversation. There is something about her that reminds him of an aging actress who has decided to take the natural road to the golden yonder, not afraid that the afternoon light is highlighting her sagging jawline.

There is a certain elegance about her, as if she has just stepped out of some chic salon. He always looks when she isn't aware. Stealing a little peek when her nose is buried in some book that she routinely brings each Saturday.

He tries not to focus as she folds her wet clothes. Putting them in an over-sized blue Ikea bag. Her undergarments are what gets him. It's as if she's given up. One little granny, two little grannies. So many grannies piled in a row.

He imagines her in high-end lingerie. A pastel pink number with her straight hair, once blonde, trailing down her back. He concentrates on the flimsy silk fabric moving just a hint from the open window. Little beads of sweat grace her forehead.

As she exits, he notices she has dropped one of her undies. Nevertheless, he can't bring himself to go after her. He is only capable of placing the garment on top of her favourite machine.

BASTA

The end is near. At least, that's what everyone is saying. Global warming, extinction, sinking cities and all the rest have been a constant on the world's tongue. Still, whom are they kidding? Lottie knows it's already here. She recently stopped working and is leaving everything that is familiar. In the last six months she has researched the more affordable places to live on a limited pension and has settled on Abruzzo, Italy, located on the Adriatic Sea, which is considered the greenest region in Europe and endowed with beautiful beaches. The lovely Rome is a mere two and half-hour drive away.

She never owned a home. Always rented. Hinged within such close proximity to neighbours that she could practically feel their breath. Recording their footsteps, music and voices. Now she wants a detached space of her own and has settled on a run-down farmhouse on the outskirts of Villa Santa Maria. It is worn and two storeys, but she adores its exterior brick walls and decent sized lot. She even has an olive grove. If the world starts to submerge, at least she is high in the mountains.

There is a large garden facing the back. The kitchen has been somewhat modernized with a recently installed gas oven and new countertops. The cupboards are old and weathered and she likes them as is. The cellar has a fireplace with chopped wood and old glass bottles line the shelves and floor. Abandoned vessels for oil and wine.

One room off the kitchen has a vaulted ceiling with exposed wood and it makes the living room feel airy and inviting. A fireplace is the main heat source for this level and above. All of the windows have wooden shutters. On the left side of the house the second floor hosts a generous landing with a large master suite and full bathroom. Upstairs there is also a vaulted ceiling with exposed wood and a double window that looks out upon the soft fields and hills beyond.

One might think she is out of her mind to settle for this seasoned house, but she had always lived in expensive dumps in the city. This feels like a palace. Somewhere she can move about, shout or do whatever comes to mind. Lottie knows rudimentary Italian. She had started and continues a course on Babbel. This will be the third country she has lived in over the last thirty-five years where her first language is not her own. The first was Amsterdam, then Montreal, now Italy. Her Dutch had been acceptable, French not so much, and now, another romantic voice to conquer.

Lottie is not gifted in diction. Yet, Italian has always been her favourite of languages. Perhaps, early on, she was seduced by all those Antonioni films. There is a passion in the lilt, the way the words dance. Oh... and the men. Looking around, she felt as if she was home, even though she had never stepped foot in this part of the world.

She didn't come with much. A few suitcases. In fact, she had sold everything before the move. She wanted a fresh start without objects of memory. All sentiment left behind on the banks of a distant sea. She had, however, bought a violin before the move. Lottie had always felt somewhat inadequate because she had never learned an instrument.

Lottie loves the violin. It is compact and she has given it a prominent place in the salon close to the music stand. She had begun a few lessons back in Montreal, but truthfully, like French, it is quite out of her grasp. Yet, Lottie is stubborn and will continue to pluck at its strings even if it kills her.

The house is stocked with old dishware, pots and utensils. Eventually she will buy a few additions to mark her own touch. There are flowers overflowing in the garden and she picks a carefree bouquet to add freshness to the kitchen. She bought an old green Fiat for getting around, one that she isn't attached to, especially if someone bumps into it or scrapes its side without leaving a courtesy note. She already feels like a citizen.

When she meets local folk she will say, *Ciao, mi chiamo Lottie.* She was named after her grandmother and detested the name as she was constantly teased at school. Lottie, snotty, potty and the list goes on... However, Lottie is her bestowed and so it sticks. Perhaps the natives will find her name exotic.

Lottie ventures into town at least four times a week to buy groceries, take in the sights, check out the inhabitants and practice her Italian. She posts an advertisement in the post office offering to sell her olives for a cheap price. Her grove has about two hundred healthy trees. Hell, what is she supposed to do with them? It is September and the harvest season will begin later in the fall.

She thinks about how nice it would be for people to come and visit in her newfound country, but, truth be told, there isn't one soul. She is an only child and her parents died when she was young. She became more of a loner in later years and her few 'acquaintances' had long given up on her. She has long suffered from the affliction of the 'gloomy gene', taking refuge in books and wine. It worries her a bit that she has settled into territory where delicious wine is inexpensive and plentiful. On the other hand, she thinks to herself, *What the fuck, can't I have something?*

Three weeks after posting the offering of her olives she receives a call.

"Buongiorno, è Vito. Come stai?"

"Ciao, Vito, Sto bene grazie."

Vito, who speaks English as if it was his first language, jumps in after hearing Lottie's heavy accent.

"Hello again. I'm Vito and I am interested in purchasing your olives. Are they still available?"

"Yes, they are. So glad someone wants to take them off my hands. There's just too many for me to manage."

"Well, I realize we're just shy of harvest, but can I come over to inspect your trees?"

"Of course."

Lottie provides Vito with directions and she begins to prepare a light lunch for his arrival. He had told her that olive production had been in his family for generations and that he believes he knows the house by her description. When he arrives, he climbs out of his pickup and stands still only turning ever so slightly to take in the perimeter of the property.

Lottie comes out smiling with an outstretched hand. He is a handsome fellow, though much younger than she, and the sheer sexuality that pours from him makes her blush in the afternoon heat.

"Hello, Lottie. Vito."

He extends his hand in return and smiles, pointing to the house.

"Yes, Yes. I thought this was the place. He goes on to tell her that the original owners had been friends with his family way back and when the parents died the children had no interest in keeping the place. One lives in Milan and the other in America.

"Yup, I'm sure I will like your olives. This place has good soil. My parents sometimes bought from this farm. Shall we examine the trees?"

They walk to the grove and he picks an olive. It is plump and healthy. After they settle on a price, Lottie invites Vito for a light lunch.

Lottie has created a quaint sitting area outside the house. There is an old trellis with a grapevine, flowers winding affectionately around it. A table has been pleasantly set with a bouquet of fresh flowers. A pitcher of iced lemon water, salad, sliced bread and prosciutto await. Wine is ready to pour. A string quartet drifts from the open house creating an atmosphere both smooth and provocative.

He settles in one of the outdoor chairs that is relaxing and easy on the back. A light breeze swoons the yard and at this precise moment all seems well in the world. At this junction Lottie decides to become someone else. Vito begins with a history lesson of the region. She listens, all the while creating a different Lottie. She is in a distant land. Why not be new too?

She does not wish to expose her past life as a woman who led an uninteresting life. Working at an insurance firm, adjusting and investigating claims. No. Nor did she want to disclose that her cousin had raised dogs for fighting and had spent several stints in prison.

Vito sits regal in the afternoon light.

"What made you move here, Lottie?"

"Well, I wanted a change and a place to recover."

"Recover? From what?"

"An accident. You see, I used to be a violinist, but since the incident I can't remember how to play and my hands and arms play havoc. I wanted to come to a place where I could start anew. I certainly don't expect my musical skills to return to what they were, however if I manage to grasp just a little…"

Even though she is much older than he, she feels his eyes bore into her. Could it be disbelief at her tale or is it a sign of tenderness?

It had been a pattern with Lottie. Attempting to mold herself into another persona in various countries. Pretending she was something she wasn't. There had always been this cloud of unworthiness. Of plainness and the ordinary. When she lived in Amsterdam she wanted to be one of those she had met who bloomed from a classical background. She remembered visiting one of her friend's family gatherings where everyone played an instrument. Shit, one of them sang opera. As she listened to the tenor she had images of her cousin and his barking, suffering hounds. How she hated him and all he stood for. Yet, she was from the same stock.

She had changed her style of dress in each place she settled. Morphing into the thread of the land. In Amsterdam she wore bright coloured short leather jackets with fashionable boots and a lot of black. In Montreal she drew on her Amsterdam influences. Now she was here living in a rural farmhouse with no one to impress but her garden.

Lottie keeps herself in shape with a regular regimen of Pilates, spot weights, and vigorous walking. She tends her garden, removing overgrown roots, adding new flowers and plants to create something more akin to her own tastes. She begins to drink wine in the early afternoon until well into the evening, often stopping to pick up her bow. Usually, by this time, she's ventured into some other state and actually thinks her playing is good. When she lays down her violin there is a serenade of hounds crying in the near distance. *"BASTA!"* can be heard from shouting neighbours beyond. Yet, she isn't sure which neighbour or from what farm the bellows chime.

Since Vito has visited her home she thinks about him steadily. As she slices her tomatoes she envisions him whisking her off to his farm, feasting on his culinary delights, deciding which design is better suited to his olive oil packaging. And... And.

Of late, when she visits the nearby village, she overhears folk talking about crops going bad. Old widows crying over an old curse from way back, when Leonardo the bad violinist made the olives fail. Now the olives are literally falling off the trees, too weak to hold on. Once, when she was in a specialty shop, she noted two men discussing some god-awful racket that was making their dogs cry at night. It sounded as if a cat was being swung by its tail.

"Si, credo che sia il suono di un violino!"

Vito is coming today. She has cleaned her house and prepared a lunch, which is sure to impress. Hell, she even took a few cooking classes in town to upgrade her skillset. The table is set in the large kitchen, the windows open, inviting a warm breeze to circulate. The smell of her spaghetti sauce lingers outside. She is hoping to impress Vito upon his arrival. First they'll eat lunch, catch up, and then she will assist him and tackle the grove.

Lottie hears his truck from far away, the wheels on the dirt road turning against the hardened earth. She smiles to herself, envisioning his handsome face and lean physique. His body chiselled into perfection from hallowed genes and hard work. She waits for him as his car enters her driveway.

"Hi, Vito."

She smiles and flattens her apron simultaneously.

"Ciao, Lottie."

She notices his serious face and asks him how he is.

"Well, this year the harvest is bad. All of the farmers are having the same problem with their crops. The olives are shriveled and not worth the pick. Even your olives won't save the bank this year."

"Oh, I'm very sorry to hear that. This is terrible."

"Well, we haven't seen it this poor in many a year, but you know everything is possible with farming."

"I've made a nice lunch. Why don't you come in and have a bite? Take your mind off things."

"Thanks, but I won't be staying. I have a meeting with the other producers. Perhaps we'll have to ask for a government loan to keep things afloat."

Lottie sadly watches his truck disappear around the bend. She enters her house and examines the well-set table. She picks up her violin and attempts to play Sonata No. 5 in F minor by Bach. After a few strings, she stops and hears Vito's voice trailing in the distance.

"È ABBASTANZA, FANCULO!"

End of Ratpure

The gold-painted angel fell today. His ceramic limbs splayed all around. She should feel saddened by this, as it was given to her in a time of love when she lived in the Dutch capital. Handed to her by her former lover who had ripped it off the exterior of an Italian villa when he was playing there in a travelling quartet.

It has made her bitter. Staring at it year after year for more than thirty. She has many objects from Amsterdam strategically placed in her flat. Often a guest will inquire, "Oh, how lovely, where did you get it?" Amsterdam.

For many years she had boasted that she had lived there feeling like she had an edge up for the experience. She kept her Dutch language books on deck ready to brush up before travelling back more than twenty times, rolling her G's and toning her tongue to Nederland standards. She constantly thought of her former lovers who became good friends, but of late had wandered far from her.

Tourists always irked the Dutch. When she had inhabited its tiny streets more than three decades ago, they had annoyed them then. Yet, she had been able to blend in like an Amsterdammer. She remembered travelers that came for smack holidays. Seeing many a folk retching on cobbled streets. One doesn't witness this now. On her last visit it made her nervous. Crowds tightly packed like little fish in a can. Tourists are more loathed now. Pouring into the small cafés, cluttering the squares. Boisterous Brits on bachelor stags.

When she had lived among the locals she had tried to absorb their mirth. Listening to them sing while riding their bicycles along the canals. Now bikes are full of danger. With cyclists roaring along texting, not a single eye on the road.

She felt a pride that she had retained her Dutch. And for the most part, Amsterdammers are happy to spar with her broken words. Still, during her last trip, when she sat at a small theatre café and left a decent tip, she had overheard the bartender turn the name, tourist, around like it was a cancer.

She has many framed photographs of her former lovers, but it pains her to hang them on the walls. They sit, hidden, in an old armoire waiting to be dismantled. Yet, she can never bring herself to complete this task. She immortalized them in print during their shared time in Amsterdam, but they never stole a peek.

So, when she looks around at hints of her Dutch past it is as if a knife sears her heart. She can't imagine strolling the streets, sitting on a sidewalk terrace, seeing the ghosts of her past. And besides, she would be just another tourist in Amsterdam.

THE WAYWARD COLLECTIVE

It began as an idea like most things. Wanda always knew, even at times of uncertainty, that she would head back east upon retirement. This notion had pulled her back like a rip tide, a true force, which she didn't have a single drop of control over. Perry, her best friend, always said, "You'll never see me there. I won't even visit." And yet he came a year later with his ornery beast, a calico cat named Mimi-Lulu.

Wanda has inherited an old house in a small seaside town. It is rundown, but Wanda, who has an innate sense of taste and order, has managed, since her return eight months ago, to convert it into an unquestionably inviting abode. And, even though the weather-bleached exterior shingles are missing here and there, most importantly, the interior modifications didn't cost an arm and a leg.

Money, or lack of it, is why she's here. The house is hers and rent-free and it is the first time in her life she can live without worrying about unaffordable apartments. She only has to pay the taxes and repairs that, unfortunately, consistently appear as shells on a beach. So, when Perry arrives it is a relief. More gravy to the pot.

Wanda's neighbour, Iris, has a beautiful garden and has given Wanda multiple clippings from her ample brood: Hollyhocks, Lilies, Lavender, Black-eyed Susans to name a few. Iris initially felt sorry for Wanda as she watched her struggle with the overgrown yard. Wanda had hoped to develop a new friendship, but Iris never once invited her over. Not even for a cup of tea. Iris is Dutch and came here as a young girl and is somewhat standoffish. She is a widow and although not what one would call a born and bred local, she considers Wanda an outsider just as the locals feel about Iris.

The house is located on a quiet road amongst blueberry bushes and a bay. It has two woodstoves, five bedrooms, wooden floors throughout and Wanda has repainted it with a lively palette of beachy colours. There is a covered porch on three sides. The second floor has three jetties. One with a peaked roof and windows on all three sides that salutes the front of the house. There are also right and left jetties, which host bedrooms and a dormer.

The entire ground and second floor have expansive windows providing the tired house with limitless sunlight. A large rambling yard faces the front and left side of house that borders Iris's garden. A wired and heated outbuilding rests in the back of the property, which Perry has requested as his studio. Perry insisted he would only come if the outbuilding could be his.

Wanda is ecstatic that Perry is here. She has been rather lonely since her return. The folk are friendly enough in the shops; nonetheless she hasn't made any new friends. Perry has brought a few trunks, one for his sculpting tools, one for bits and bobs. The minute he enters the house Wanda attempts to pat Mimi-Lulu, but she only hisses and scratches Wanda's outstretched hand.

"Well, some things never change."

"Oh, Wanda, she's just scared."

Wanda lets Perry choose his own bedroom. Hers is upstairs and her windows face the front and sides of the yard as if she is the captain of a ship, which is sort of true. Perry decides on the downstairs bedroom close to the bathroom. There are three other bedrooms upstairs. Mimi-Lulu has disappeared and probably will only surface for Perry. She has always been unfriendly and only has eyes for him.

Perry is pleased with his studio. He had once been anointed with the glaze of celebrity in the nineties with a spread about his work in *ARTnews* and various other art journals. He had a few group shows and a solo with modernist galleries. Stubbornly, he has stuck to his subject that revolves around the phallus and throughout the years his devotees who wished to see another artistic path have abandoned him, and causing his notoriety to shrunk as if it were itself a limp member.

He had been teased by mean name-calling when he was a boy at school. Perry is a fairy, poofter and so on. Also, he had been persecuted by his own father and in reaction to all of this, Perry came out very early and there is an atmosphere of the dramatic about him. This testimony to male sexuality is at the very core of his artistry and he immediately begins investigating where to buy supplies to get a new series of sculptures on the go.

Perry and Wanda go a long ways back and often their evenings are spent drinking wine and reminiscing about their former wild adventures: Go-go dancing on Perry's small city balcony after a dinner party, Perry's preference for men of shorter stature, the many concerts and endless parties they attended and sometimes when they've had too much, they put on the Sex Pistols or the B-52's and have a dance, despite stiff joints and bad knees.

It has taken time for Perry to embrace his new surroundings, for he is a city boy and finds this quiet place hard on his nerves. Still, the roominess of the house and his own private workspace has won him over, for a studio would have been unattainable had he remained in Montreal. Money is what it boils down to. It is what grants freedom or restraint.

A couple of months following Perry's arrival, the plumbing goes awry when Wanda is bathing and Perry is doing the dishes. The house has galvanized pipes that must be replaced. The sediment is so thick from build-up throughout the years that only a few drops escape from the pipes. It is decided that new lodgers are required to help with the bills. Perry and Wanda don't like this idea one bit, but can find no other way out. She places an advertisement on craigslist and in the local shops. Three soon materialize.

The first is Dot. She likes the idea of companionship. Insufficient savings is also a driving force that propels her to the idea of community living. She had worked for the SPCA most of her life and is an animal lover.

"Oh there's a cat here! Great."

However, when Mimi-Lulu comes out of hiding for a drink of water and Dot extends her hand, Mimi-Lulu only hisses as she raises her head from her dish.

Japamala is the second. Her real name is Denise, however she has adopted Japamala as her own. She is a yoga lover, has spirited blue eyes and travels the world when she is flush visiting yoga retreats.

"The yard is beautiful. I'll give yoga lessons out there, weather permitting of course." Her toned body brims with enthusiasm.

The third is Ethan, or Taffy as he is often called. Ethan was a roofer and always tanned a creamy bronze the colour of the chewy candy. He is wrinkled, walks with a limp, uses a cane subequent to a fall and was on disability until his pension kicked in. Nonetheless he has kept in shape and there is a sexual allure about him despite his weathered skin. He holds a seductive sloping grin like Sam Elliott when his face is still. Even Perry finds him attractive.

All three roomies move in shortly after. Dot and Japamala come first and each choose the east and west rooms upstairs. Ethan takes the room in the back of the house, which has a clear view of Iris's house. Initially, they have a house meeting deciding whether to eat together, who does what chores in the yard and house. Dot goes first.

"I'm happy to do yard work. I like to be amongst the birds."

"I'm not interested in being part of a household chore schedule. Everyone take care of their own shit." Perry heads out to his studio.

"OK, we're all in agreement then. Each of us is responsible for our own messes."

Wanda stands up first as if she's the chair of this board meeting and heads to the kitchen. "Who wants tea?"

Perry used to work with marble, but has recently changed to fiberglass resin. It is less expensive and he likes the idea of bold colour, a deviation from his former creative executions. While the roomies are sorting themselves out in their new surroundings, Perry can be heard banging, sawing and chipping away. Loud music escapes the outdoor studio. 'I Wanna Be Your Dog', by the Stooges assaults Iris's ears as she is burrowing up an eager raspberry bush whose roots had spread like wildfire.

Of late there is a heaviness in the air since the house has been revived. It had been vacant for some time before Wanda and this new clan had moved in. As the morning fogs lifts Perry installs colossal primary-coloured penis sculptures in her direct field of vision. Some are erect and proud, while one is shy or sleepy and the other is inquisitive as if a periscope from a submerged submarine scouring the horizon for possible action. When Iris returns to hoeing, she wishes she were digging a mass grave for the whole lot of them.

Initially, Wanda's household decided on having a communal evening meal together. Each taking a turn cooking throughout the week, but this hasn't worked out, as Japamala is a vegetarian and on several occasions the meal was made without consideration for her dietary disapprovals. She won't consider anything which had been cooked in a pot where meat had been sizzled. Perry is fussy with his culinary tastes and disliked all of the meals that had been prepared by the others. Especially Dot. He never tasted anything so bland and blah.

Ethan eats out most evenings. He goes to the pub and throws back a few. He hankers fish and chips and often stops by Mod's Cod or the town diner. He isn't much of a cook anyways, although Dot tries to woo him with her breakfasts often enough. Sometimes Ethan obliges, slowly chewing, lifting an eyebrow while Dot smiles, rubbing her hands down her pear like shape waiting approval.

Japamala also vies for Ethan's attention. Stretching her slim form whenever he is in sight. Regularly, she offers up a non-coniferous dish with the hope of... well she isn't quite sure. Nonetheless he certainly appeals to her. She has bought her own set of cookware insisting they are off limits. The others agree without complaint. Ironically, they are a deep red, the semblance of blood.

Within the month things in the house have been rearranged. Utensils, dishes, glasses and furniture are placed in symmetrical and perfect order. One day when Perry was in town he came back to find all his tools and paints had been repositioned as if it were an army barracks. Even the bath towels have been reshuffled according to length and tint intensity, although each of them has their own identifiable hook.

Iris notices every evening the blinds in Ethan's room go up and down and the lights turn on and off for several consistent intervals. She wonders if he is sending her some kind of erotic message. But truth be told, he only has eyes for Iris's garden, for he envisions uprooting all of her plants and replanting them according to height, colour and curvaceousness.

"Alright, who's been fucking with my studio? I don't appreciate the clean up." Perry knows it isn't Wanda. She's far too lazy for such things.

It is unusual that they are all in the kitchen at one time.

"Well, it certainly isn't me!" Dot and Japamala shout in unison.

"Then it must be you, Taff, or should I say Ethan?

"It is. I'm afraid I can't help myself. I've had this problem since I can remember. I thought it would please everyone."

"We know your intentions are kind, but leave things as they are. Especially my studio, there is a system in my mess."

"No problem, Perry. I'll stay clear."

"And besides, none of us wants our wash clothes all mixed up. Think of the germ transfers. Who knows where Wanda's ol' puss has been?"

Wanda and Perry laugh hysterically nearly wetting themselves, while the others feel violated at the mere thought of Wanda's private parts.

"OK then, who wants a drink?" Perry has a Margaritaville and prepares drinks for himself, Wanda and Ethan. Dot and Japamapla decline and he thinks, *Excellent! More for us.* Mimi-Lulu rests at the base of Perry's feet glaring at the others with complete disapproval.

Since Ethan is good with his hands, Dot asks him to build her some birdhouses. She is secretly in love with him and thinks it will curb his yen for order. As he inspects the grounds for best direction and placement Japamala stretches on the lawn. She arches her body like a cat and does the wide-legged forward bend with her legs spread and her butt positioned high in the air. Even her scantily-clad yoga class newbies are incapable of averting his attention. Ethan is preoccupied with the trees, imagining the birdhouses all harmoniously hanging equal distance and height within the branches. All the while Mimi-Lulu skulks in the bushes observing Ethan suspending each pied-à-terre.

It didn't take long before dead birds were left at the front door. On one occasion there was a dead baby bunny. Dot, who cherishes all animals, is beginning to loathe Mimi-Lulu and, although she hasn't witnessed this carnage, she knows without a doubt it's her.

Dot is consistently the first one up. As she prepares coffee she hears a sequence of short, but loud, sharp peeps. The kitchen windows are open and the birdhouses can be clearly observed from the window above the sink.

Dot abandons her coffee and runs out to inspect what's going on. As she approaches one of the birdhouses there is a panicked sparrow trapped within by one of the paws of Mimi-Lulu.

The second she moves in, Mimi-Lulu lunges at Dot, scratching her arms before hitting the ground and making a beeline for Perry's studio. The sparrow exits, heading for the sky all the while chirping in protest, its fragile form becoming a mere speck on the horizon. Three abandoned eggs rest in a nest. Dot marches into Perry's bedroom where he is deep in sleep, snoring like a Warthog.

"Your cat is evil!"

"Ugh? I was asleep. What do you want?"

"I said your cat is horrid, wicked. Whatever adjective you prefer. I never imagined I'd say this about an animal."

Perry rubs his eyes, watching a droplet of blood drip down Dot's clawed arm.

"She's always been an indoor kitty. Let her have some fun for fuck sake."

And in that instant an unexpected phrase from a Seinfeld episode pops into Perry's head.

"Serenity now!"

Dot slams the door and returns to the kitchen.

"Wanda. What are we going to do about Dot?"

"What do you mean?"

"I can't stand her. She's gotta go. And Japamala, fuck I hate her stupid name, is getting on my nerves too. With her nose out of joint every time I roast a chicken or grill a steak."

"Yeah. Well... we just can't kick them out."

"I know, but I can't take those two for one more minute."

Things have been rather gloomy around the house. Japamala hasn't recruited any additional yoga students. The weather has been wet and laced with heavy fog for most of the summer and this has not proven attractive for newbies to stretch on soggy grass. As everyone is mingling around the kitchen, Perry proposes, *Let's have a party*.

"What do you think? Summer will be over in a breath. There are long faces in this house. We can invite some town folk. What do you say?"

"Whatever" seems to be the general mood at the suggestion as they exit the kitchen. Wanda is the only one excited by the idea.

"Town folk? What folks, Perry? Iris is the only one we know."

"Speak for yourself, Wanda. I've met a few furballs."

"You haven't."

"I have. Wanda, do you seriously expect I'd be able to tolerate this uneventful town if there wasn't the occasional rub-a-dub-dub?"

"You're too much."

"I'm just saying... And I even have shrooms."

"Really! How did you get them?"

"I have my sources."

Wanda and Perry laugh like hyenas that just had a kill, clinking their coffee mugs in the morning light.

The following Saturday is the chosen evening for the party. The weather predicts dry and pleasantly warm conditions and there will be a full moon. Perry and Wanda string lights and place candles in every conceivable nook and cranny. They have made a couple long tables out of old doors and sawhorses. Wanda covers them with white sheets and twilight falls. An atmosphere of calmness settles over the yard. The odd firefly dancing against the coming night highlights the teal-coloured sky. To be polite and the fact there will be a party and noise, Wanda extends an invitation to Iris.

"Iris, we'd be delighted if you'd join us for the evening."

She accepts with the true intention of confronting them about the penis sculptures, which infuriate her.

"Well… it's very kind of you. Yes, perhaps I'll come."

"Perry. Do you think we should tell everyone about the mushrooms?"

"No. Why?"

"But, if we don't and someone has a bad trip…"

"Come on, everyone has fun on shrooms."

"OK then, but we'll just put small amounts in the balls. Let me at least make a place card with a message… have a nice flight."

Before everyone arrives, Perry and Wanda put out food plates of prepared cheeses, breads, crackers, olives, pates and cold cuts. The shrooms are wrapped in a layer of peanut butter, perfectly symmetrical and tempting with the little card on top of the tray of balls. Perry and Wanda have already chowed down on rather generous portions and have become somewhat unhinged each time they address one another. Laughing excessively over the simplest of things.

Dot eyes them with suspicion and Japamala who had forty minutes ago swallowed a ball, begins stretching and dancing on the recently mowed lawn smiling like the Cheshire Cat. Sometimes cementing her hands on the grass staring at the ground for prolonged periods of time. Ethan also partakes in multiple shroom balls and when Iris arrives he is all smiles and outstretches his hand.

"Welcome, I'm Ethan."

"Hello. Iris."

"I've been admiring your garden."

"Oh… have you now?"

Iris nervously bites into a ball drumming up the courage to go one-on-one regarding the sculptures. The card is no longer visible and has fallen on the ground. Not long after Iris pops a shroom the party is in full swing and Perry's two furball friends arrive. Wanda, Perry and his two gentleman callers are soon in deep conversation.

"Can you believe it? I'm getting a show. The dazzling dicks are a hit."

They all clap and chuckle until they're attention is averted to Japamala twirling about the yard again, often hesitating for and extended period of time staring at some undetermined point of interest.

"What's up with those two?"

As they watch, Dot turns her head in every direction as if she is attempting to decode some alien transmission.

"I don't know. I wish they'd move out."

Dot appears uneasy and peeps into the bushes and trees imagining sounds and animals in distress, sometimes disappearing for lengths of time. Ethan introduces Iris to the others and just before Iris can open her mouth Perry, Wanda and the furballs erupt in laughter. Their diaphragms contracting as they gasp for breath between hysterical outbursts.

"I don't know what is so comical. Now, about those sculptures… I really don't know how you expect me to tolerate them. I'm forced to look at them from every angle of my house and garden."

"Come on, they're fun. I think they liven up the place. Well, someone appears to appreciate them. I'm getting a show."

Just as Iris is about to respond, Ethan takes her arm and pivots her in the direction of her garden, yet Iris feels nauseous and stops, thinking she will be sick to her stomach. By the time they reach the yard's border Iris is light in the head and her vision is altered when she looks at her porch with its strung white lights running the length of the veranda. The moon is shimmering in the night sky with several rings of light surrounding it.

"I feel strange. Was something in the drinks?"

"Perry made shroom balls and we all had a bit. Don't worry, all will be well. It won't last forever."

"Well they could have warned me first."

Ethan and Iris sit on the bench in her garden and he suggests various ways in which the flowers could be changed. For instance, instead of mixed hues, why not arrange all according to height and colour. The more he goes on the more Iris is open to his ideas. Iris collects her spades and shovels and they immediately get down to work forgetting about the party. Rows of whites, reds, yellows, blues and the odd purple and pinks have all been uprooted and replanted. The flowers seem delighted with their new arrangements. Some seem to smile.

At one point their digging is interrupted by a loud shriek. Dot comes dashing out of the bushes with her face covered in blood after stumbling upon Perry and the furballs partaking in a threesome. Just as she makes a run for it, Mimi-Lulu launches from a tree branch scratching her face before hitting the ground and dashing away.

"Perry, your fucking cat clawed me again!"

"Oh she can be a naughty kitty." Perry's chuckled words becoming evermore distant.

As Dot runs towards the yard, Wanda averts her target by grabbing her arm and forcing her to sashay around the yard to the tunes of The Buzzcocks. Nevertheless, Dot breaks away dashing to the house and is not seen for the remainder of the soiree.

When dawn breaks, Ethan and Iris have worked for hours. They are covered with dirt and the yard looks as if it is in severe shock. There are piles and holes and noticeably stressed stems. Iris tries to grasp her decision to undertake this endeavour that the evening before had seemed so sound.

Distracted when they hear a door slam, they notice Japamala and Dot heading to their cars, arm and arm with numerous suitcases. They had discussed well into the night the unsettling vibe of this very household, deciding it was not for them a minute longer. Mere seconds later, Iris turns her attention to her war-torn oasis. Tears run down her face like a warm summer shower. Ethan takes his worked hand and wipes one away. Waiting for another and another.

Skin

I sit at a terrace of an outside café. A sizable potted plant diffuses the sunlight, yet it feels like I could fry an egg on my forearm. I watch the gazelles stroll along the boardwalk, their compositions gleaming in the midday sheen. These garlanded creatures look festive with their tattooed hides. The eye can get lost within an abstraction, symbol or text.

I wonder what they'll do when one grows tired of a lover's monogram. A sacred message that no longer holds truth or a likeness of a place and time they wish to forget.

I examine my old skin in the shadowed light, which has the appearance of tired lace. What will become of those body modifications when the dyes and pigments no longer hold their veneers? When the skin has reached its zenith? Illustrated epidermis dissolving into unrecognizable disorder.

For now I drink their mirth. Observing as they caress arms and legs. Lifting a shirt to display a hidden brand. Age will be upon them one day. Burnished skin will be their foe. Will they cover the fatigued semblances with long sleeves and slacks or proudly flaunt them with faltering limbs?

Proost

It's cozy and the atmosphere is warm and intoxicating. She loves the Amsterdam Cafés. This one dates back to the sixteenth century and it feels natural to sit here. A part of the world which was once her home.

She examines the patrons and catches the glimpse a man roughly the same age as herself. He sits next to a large, elongated antique window with a series of circles in the lower panes. She wonders what he is thinking...

He's attractive and she imagines how it would be to sleep with him. She frames the scene in her head and orders another drink. Time has amassed since she's been with someone and she's far from certain how her body will perform.

She stares off into the soft-lit space all the while repeating Kegels for fifteen count intervals. It is a secret task that no one can detect. The bartender lights candles along the bar and she thinks of her neighbourhood and the many Northern cardinals who sing in the tree outside her flat looking for dates.

The man she's been eyeing comes to her and invites her to his place. She is pleased to accept hoping she can make it there without incident echoing her Kegels, trying not to lose a drop along the way.

FLIPSIDE

She had a system. It had proved to be a useful tool throughout her life, which is near the closer end of finish. She had kept the same mundane job, which bored her to death, yet stuck to it because it had a skimpy pension plan. She settled in the same crap rental for countless years in order to harvest affordable living increases, even though the neighbours came and went, and with them her nerves. Continually adjusting to new inhabitants with their noises and particularities. Often, she felt like packing herself up in a box and mailing it off to some unknown exciting location.

Now things will change. She is heading back east. A place she hasn't lived for forty years. Sure, she has visited countless times; nevertheless, she is wary of her homecoming. Hell, she doesn't even know anyone there anymore. However, the sea beckons her.

If one is from these parts the blue is hardwired. Something that calls you back, something you can't resist. Something so full of desire one can never resist its briny wet kiss. Now she's left a place she has lived for most of her adult life, and from years of hoarding, has been able to buy a humble abode in a place she has never been. The price was good and it has a sea view, but conveniences are far away.

She was accustomed to have all that is necessary within walking distance. Great specialty shops, pharmacy, hardware to name a few. Now she is solitary amongst fog and multi-coloured Lupins, a large rambling yard that she knows will be too much upkeep and a lengthy driveway that will prove laborious with dense snowfall. She has put herself in surroundings that go against all before.

She doesn't know a soul here and there isn't even a shop to post a note for a handyman. She looks online, but small towns are far away. She is fussy when it comes to atmosphere and likes her things placed in a aesthetically pleasing fashion. Still, items must be installed. She gets out her electric drill and begins organizing fifteen wooden shelves to be mounted on one white wall.

They must be mathematically calculated so that they will be even and symmetrical. She grabs a few screw fasteners while standing on a stool and starts from the highest point. Each time she attempts to install a fastener, the old wall crumbles as if riddled by machinegun fire.

Framed glass-encased photographs that she obsessively rearranges in order of history, sentiment and lost youth are strewn across the floor. These recordings of time make her feel less isolated as if she is enveloped amongst old lovers and friends. She eyeballs the frames and marks the wall with a thin pencil point, however once installed they are entirely uneven and another wall has been peppered with small nail holes.

She lets out a slow moan looking in the antique mirror resting upon her great grandmother's Mahogany bureau. *Fuck, Izzy, what was in your head? Why did you come back here?* But she has moved here and must make the best of it. All order blown away as if taken by the North Atlantic's ornery winds and beginning to feel as if a bad omen has descended on her modest seaside home.

Izzy never drove, but has maintained her license by paying the yearly fee. She had been too nervous to drive in Montreal with its angry, aggressive drivers, but here she needs a car and hit Kijiji, buying one quickly. She naively took the word of the seller that it is, in fact, a good car. He was simply selling because he required a larger vehicle.

The mileage is reasonable and he provided invoices of recent brake work and oiling. Even a set of winter tires were part of the deal. She drives home taking the back roads to get comfortable with the car and, although she hears strange sounds from the engine, Izzy feels free, perhaps for the first time in her life.

Winter comes early. November swooped in with all its gloomy might and with it—snow. At least twelve centimeters have fallen and no end in sight when Izzy looks out from her kitchen window. She hasn't bothered to buy a shovel yet and curses herself for procrastination. Her car is close to the house and she will need to sweep and grab a dustpan to be able to access the road, which will likely take hours. By the time Izzy has cleared the drive she is close to collapse. Totally surprised that she hasn't dropped dead on the spot from a coronary. Imagining that someone would discover her in the spring half-eaten by maggots. A sad little tale that will stick to these shoreline folk like a starfish to a rock.

She shakes the idea from her head and looks up at her house with its blue shingles and white vinyl siding melting into the snowy backdrop. She feels lonely here with only the wind nipping at her face. Her feet half frozen to the ground. Smoke from the woodstove rises above the darkened clouds as if trying to escape to an uncharted solar system. With her cold feet she returns to her home realizing that the steppingstones she has journeyed were unsound. Isolating herself in this companionless part of the world.

The home was to have been her haven, but it is a mess with tools, shelves and frames scattered across the rooms. She can't even watch television or Netflix, as it will be another week before the Internet is connected. Never imagining in a thousand lifetimes this scenario when she was living in a city far away. There isn't one yummy morsel to eat. As she stands before her living room window she looks to the sea, ominous and unforgiving.

The following day Izzy drives to the nearest town to buy groceries: wine, beer and a carton of cigarettes. On the return trip she hears grinding and clicking reminiscent of her father's workshop with its drills and planers. Jointers and table saw. Lathe. Envisioning all the machines working in a fury as she drives along the coastline. Without a doubt, there is a major problem with the car and she curses the seller—wishing him erectile dysfunction and anal warts!

She hasn't been to the beach yet. Locals say it is the most beautiful beach in Nova Scotia. Izzy loves a beach, but then who doesn't? She is especially drawn to the deserted ones at this time of the year with limited light and a sombre tone. She hopes the solitude will center her. She wishes to touch her seclusion. Taste it. Try to decode her reasoning for immersing herself in these surroundings. Inhabiting a house full of messes and failed handy-woman executions.

If she were in the city, what would she be doing? Sitting on the sofa drinking one-too-many Coronas. Feeling her bloated belly jiggle each trip to the fridge. Wasting her time, flipping stations and fuming that HBO has become repetitive and boring and still expensive. Annoyed by the noises of her neighbours, their vacuums, televisions, music and sexual moans.

Perhaps, she would have ventured out for takeout Thai to escape them or strolled the streets. Gazing in the windows of others. Imagining their conversations and decrypting body language. Questioning, *Why do I need to live here?* Rereading *The Andy Warhol Diaries* before bed, which make her feel like a loser with her near non-social life. All the while, Andy and his consorts are whipping it up at The Factory or Studio 54 with one party after the next.

She makes a grilled cheese sandwich and sits before the living room window watching the grey sky. She thinks back to her childhood spent with her parents, cousins, aunt and uncle. Swimming in lakes at summer cottages, and before that, camping each summer. How she was always in trouble for mischievous behaviour.

Izzy remembers running from a lake to the campground ahead of her cousins and telling her aunt, who was eight months pregnant that her cousin, Lily, had drowned in the lake and her other cousin didn't know what to do, so he was just looking at her body floating in the still water with a halo of reeds circling her head.

Izzy thought this quite hilarious, though then she was very young. She upset everyone. So much, in fact, that her aunt, uncle, cousins and parents packed up their tents and headed off to their respective homes. Izzy got seriously scolded and remembered a Wild Canary hit their windshield and died on the way home. Now, all her kin have passed and there is no one left to relive these yarns.

Izzy cranks the engine and hears an awful clamour from under the hood. Undaunted she turns the beast around the drive and heads to the main road leading her to the beach. The road in is plowed to a gate, but from then onwards she must walk. She pulls onto the flattened snow and parks. The engine rattles and protests until it finally quiets and stills. She takes the long path with mounds of snow softly rising on each side. As she approaches wisps of sea grass stretch towards the sky. Others are trodden down by damp snow. Along the shoreline, where the waves break the edge, a few seagulls peck the sand. There is a loon bobbing not far from shore and its lonely call seeps deep within her. She has brought a thermos of tea and a blanket to sit on. The wind is light, but there is good surf off a point at the far left section of beach. A rock outcrop, about a quarter mile, stretches beyond the last stretch of sand and to her surprise she spies a figure on a surfboard patiently awaiting a decent wave in the dark swell. The figure occupies all her concentration as she watches, what she assumes is a man, riding wave upon wave. Izzy sits there until her tea is long gone and her feet feel frozen to the ground.

The surfer has vanished. She picks up a few beach treasures along the shoreline before heading back to her car, yet when she arrives the engine won't turn over. She curses her ignorance of motors or the inner workings of mechanics and Izzy begins to cry. She is raw and shudders at the mere thought of walking to the main road. The blanket she has brought is damp and stiff and has begun to freeze. She thinks to herself, *Fuck, I can't even call an Uber.*

As Izzy pounds the car with her fist and kicks the wheels with her near frostbitten feet she hears footsteps in the snow. A figure wearing a black wetsuit emerges from the path carrying a surfboard under his arm. He is covered in frost and a series of tiny icicles hang from his facial stubble.

"What's the trouble? Are you alright?"

Izzy cries so hard she finds it difficult to stop shaking.

"It won't start."

"Oh, that's nothing to be so upset about, now."

"You don't know the half of it. Everything here is shit."

"Come on, it can't be that bad. Why don't you come with me and get warmed up. I live very near to the beach. As a matter of fact, just up from the left side of the shore. I'll give you something to warm your bones."

Izzy gulps back her tears and agrees to follow.

"I never felt this cold in my life."

"I'm Bob, by the way."

"Hello. Izzy."

This is untrue, as she has felt miserably cold many times in Montreal with its horribly frigid, endless winters. She follows behind him on the narrow path. Up ahead stands a trailer with smoke rising from a narrow chimney pipe. She can smell the fired wood hanging in the twilight air. The sky is a deep teal and the stars have joined the night.

There is a battered sign mounted to a post in the ground, which reads "Barrels Or Bust" at the entrance to the property and a broken-down four-wheeler with two flats parked to one side. A handsome fire pit made of beach stones rests just short of the trailer and one can catch a good view of the sea. Three surfboards are piled up against an outbuilding.

As Izzy enters the door she feels at ease. Perchance it's merely the warmth of the inside air from the woodstove providing instant comfort, like a tight long-felt bear hug.

"Make yourself at home, Izzy. I'll just get this surf garb off."

Bob motions for her to sit at a table and pours a generous neat whiskey. He goes into some darkened passageway and draws a curtain. She hears snaps and assumes the quick stretch of rubber, then a shower running in the back. The trailer is rundown, but there is a homey atmosphere about it. Seashells and surf books line the living area. Pots hang from a hook on the ceiling. Bob reappears soon after with a flannel shirt and corduroy pants. He is of similar age and unquestionably attractive.

"So, Izzy, are you feeling your toes again?"

"Sort of, I mean yes. The fire and whiskey help."

He smiles at her. She notices many framed photographs of a surfer hanging on the wall and arrayed on a shelf. She sees an article, *Nova Scotia surfer "Surfer Bob" wins again*, in a framed clipping from a newspaper, and next to it a photograph of a surfer gunning the barrel of a giant wave.

"You surf! I watched you the entire afternoon. I'm amazed that you can tolerate the cold, especially at this time of the year. I grew up in Nova Scotia and even in summer it's unbearable."

"One must love it and dress accordingly. I've surfed these waters since I was a boy. Can imagine no other place I'd rather be. This spot is serene and there aren't many folk around, which suits me fine. Have you ever been on a board?"

"No. No. Not me. When I think of it, I envision warmer waters."

Bob pours Izzy another drink and tells her a little about himself.

"We'll look at your car tomorrow morning. I'm pretty good with engines. You can take the spare bed in the back."

As she looks up into the darkness through the old skylight, flurries begin to fall. They drift slowly down joining her thoughts that have settled on this stretch of shore.

What's What

Lordy, Lordy, what's the world coming to? A query always pondered. My veranda faces the sea and the beat of the waves pulse against the present. Imagine… celebrities selling candles that smell like their private parts. What will be next? And pffft… look at this one hobbling into court with a cheap walker supported by tennis balls wanting everyone to know how feeble and impoverished he is. Hope he gets many a visit in the clink by butch bikers on the quest for love.

Time slides by and the communiqués a keep a rollin'. Murders, rapes an arson or two. Terrorists and pernicious viruses travelling our sphere. Reckon, I'm lucky to be where I am with the gulls croaking and the ocean stretching far from the pulse of mainstream life.

That bully is still in office, tweeting and ranting spewing maniacal commentaries like some just released sociopath. All the coin spent on that circus could have nourished a small nation. What's to become… I'm lucky to live in this distant hamlet. Camouflaged by fog and watched over by legions of black crows that bark from tree to tree, sometimes a visit by the odd sea beast off this vast stretch on beach.

I'm back to that candle again with all the blended scents, geranium, citrus, cedar, damask rose to name a few. I'm thinking about the sort of fools who buy these products. Imagining some sorry soul sitting in a dimly lit room. The only source of light is from that candle spewing its concocted pudenda. Does he feel connected to that woman. Imagining her sitting next to him, whispering in his ear. Asking—so whatcha think?

I think it's better to stay clear of headlines, rarely a comforting word. I'll stick to brine and barnacles. What is definite and true. A foghorn and forever horizon for my daily dish.

TRANSPARENCIES

Oh... here we go again. Packing up, but hopefully the last time I recon if in truth I get there. I can't remember the number of times I've moved in my life—too many. I'm trimming my chattels 'cause my new digs are compact. Now I must decide what goes and what's tossed. I've carted and carried these Herculean bags of photographs from home to home. Let me bestow another glance. Do I even remember who's in these likenesses?

I've given the armoire to the couple next door. I don't want to lug a heavy piece like that across country. I know it's worth a few bucks, ah.... what do I care? Time is a ticking. Tickety tick. Tickety tock. I'm heading for the dock. I think about it a lot. The dock, that is. Loading my pockets with stones and taking a leap right in. I wouldn't say I'm a misery. OK, sometimes. Still, I feel like a rusty old bolt where everything hurts, seized-up from overuse and senectitude.

Now let's see, eye us fresh and full of expectation. I must be about seventeen and there's Ida and Henry. Aren't we a tasty lot? Time has had its way with us. Ida passed long ago and I have no clue whatever became of Henry. Myself, I stay well clear of mirrors now. My turn is a-coming.

First off, have a peek. Art school. I can't throw these away. I think those days were the most fun of my life. The contact sheets, black and white emulsions falling on the wooden floorboards like turned autumn leaves.

Leather and pale skin. Mohawks. Bejewelled faces and ears adorned with rings and studs. Bright eyes with hints of the devil in them. Danger. Those were the days all right. We thought we were something and I guess every generation does. Why has life become so mundane? Dull as dishwater they say from whence I hatch.

I've recorded these visual memories like a diary. So when someone becomes foggy in my recollection, I only have to pick one up and there they are whole and complete and I'm instantly living in that moment when the light, the longing and the joke was savoured like it had been in that sliver of instance.

Not sure what to pitch. Here are cousins, I think. I don't even remember their names. Out. And these ol' high school photos? Well, that's Heather, my bestie, back then. Man, she could be long dead for all I know, but I'll keep her because she meant something once. The others—sayonara.

Oh, my! Check this out—the oil patch years. There we are smoking a joint, layered in mud leaning on the hood of our truck. Those were crazy days. Working four hundred hours a month, seven days a week. Doing seismographic exploration, everyone saving for a distinct cause. I remember living deep in the bush and waiting for 'message hour' that came on the local radio somewhere far from us at the same time every afternoon. Folk lived so removed from each other that the local station put out messages for neighbours. Don't forget now, this is about fifteen years before the Internet. One could hear an announcement like:

"Fred, come pick up your yellow bucket."

"Mike. Stop shooting deer on my land."

"Hazel. Those cheddar tea biscuits were out of this world. Give me some more my lovely."

And here, we are around the sixth hour in an eight drive on a cutline through the hinterland to the nearest town when Look and Behold! A hunter with a rifle slung over his back hitchhiking, standing there in the middle of nowhere smoking a cigarette. Of course we gave him a lift to town.

Our fortress. We were lucky as children with the sea spread before us and the woods at our backs. We had it all. Treasure hunting, forts in the woods made of tree branches and old rocks. Often, a bit of cloth topped with the cool breath of emerald moss. How we played outside from morning to night, swimming, roaming. Stopping only for a quick bite. Endless days of summer with hours of playing dress up with spears made of tree branches and crowns woven of twigs and wild flowers.

Man. I thought I had destroyed all of these, yet there she is—Ophelia, smirking, staring right at me with her intense blue eyes. They never found her body, I made sure of that. I'm not proud of what I did; still ya can't shift the past. The night was humid and the sky clear bursting with stars. My mind is dimmer than it used to be yet I can remember it like it happened a mere nanosecond ago.

It was our party place deep in the woods. Far from the eyes and ears of the police. We drank, smoked reefers, often consuming other illicit substances. Hell yeah, it was the seventies and we were teenagers. Those were the days all right, full of freedom and hope. Not as now, where the world seems to be nearing the edge and there isn't a single thing to grab on to.

That particular evening Ophelia came across Alfie and me. She was what you would call—a mean girl. Always smiling with her perfect orthodontist-treated teeth as she plotted to steal someone's boyfriend or ignite a rumour about a rival. Alfie had fallen for her charms as all the boys did.

We were hanging out drinking wine and dreaming about a future, which we imagined would be more interesting than where we were sitting under the trees on that summer night. She rolled up in her sky blue Karmann Ghia convertible on the old road next to the lake. We were at the rocks with a cozy fire crackling in the ground level fire pit. We weren't allowed to make fires up there, yet we always doused it with lake water at the end of the eve. We respected the land.

I reckon Ophelia was looking for a party, because most times there was always a gang tripping out and skinny-dipping up there. She was none too pleased when she saw only Alfie and me. She started name-calling, saying I liked her sloppy seconds and firing off a slew of insults that hung in the air like the fireflies that danced against those nights.

Feast your eyes, my parents' wedding photos. What a vision. I am an only child and I never had any of my own. Who'll want to keep these? My grandmother is also there in the bridal party. She always said, Lucille, you were born on a Wednesday and Wednesday's child is full of woe don't you know?

I was a moody kid. Bored I reckon, because I was often alone having no siblings to hang with. We lived a ways out and I had a fair hoof to my playmates' homes. I had a friendly mutt named Buttercup. She was so sweet and we went everywhere together until she was killed by a pack of coyotes.

Look at her smiling for the camera with a juicy beef bone at the base of her front paws. It still can bring tears. I'll keep this one. And there's Marty, Rhonda and me on one of our canoe trips down river in middle school. We camped and spoke about our future plans, which never came to fruition. Vamoose.

Ophelia leers again in a group photo at one of our parties. I don't remember the names of the others. This one has to go. Sure, I've had interludes of remorse at times. But hey, she asked for it. Getting out of her fancy car and spewing those contemptuous remarks, well look at you two losers and so forth on that hot summer night.

Alfie and I had a couple of bottles open and she strutted over she purposely knocking them with her foot, breaking them without apology. Who gives a shit about your cheap slosh anyways, as she kicked dirt onto our fire?

It was at that precise moment I got up and pushed her. It happened in an instant. She lost her balance and fell backwards striking her blonde endowed head on a boulder. Our watering hole was a ridge of smooth and sharp bedrock with the atmosphere of an ancient monument. I knew she was dead and in that jiff I didn't feel a single drop of guilt. Then the panic set in.

Alfie started screaming and I quickly told him to hush. We had to think about what to do. His uncle was a sort of crook and had a garage where he bought and sold stolen cars. Sometimes, he just stripped them for parts. I imagine he got a tidy sum for the Karmann Ghia. He probably just repainted and sold it. I never asked.

I suggested we drive the car over to his shop once we got rid of her body. The lake was out of the equation. That was the first place the police looked. Sending the divers down there to the depths and others to the forest to scan the timbered floor.

Well, well whom do we have here? Look at us on Halloween. Happy with our pillowcases overfilled with treats, our faces brimming with mischief and delight. And there we are again, my childhood comrades, carolling on Christmas Eve. Every year there was a fight deciding who would carry the bells. The older kids in our tiny group always beat us on that one.

I don't like thinking about Ophelia. I've put her way back in the deep pockets of my mind, nevertheless re-examining this photograph I can conjure up her snarly little mouth with those oh-so-perfect pouty lips. Alfie was crazed with fear that night, but he was bound to me and I needed him. We lived in a land of lakes. Each one a short distance from the next. They couldn't explore all of them so we took her out to Sawmill Lake. It was a fair drive away and disarmingly pretty from the shore, though you wouldn't want to swim there. It had leaches the size of small snakes.

We stuffed her in the trunk and gathered some heavy rocks to load her down. Luckily enough, there was some rope in the trunk with the spare tire. We needed a boat and headed to a lake further away where cottage folk congregated on weekends. Alfie found a light, compact rowboat straight off the bat. We untied her from the dock and quickly portaged it up the hill securing it onto the roof of Ophelia's car.

Hush! Hush! Hush! I told Alfie who was driving erratically shouting and crying and stating this is the end of life as we know it. Pay attention now! We have to be clever. Once we dropped her in the middle of the lake tied to the spare tire loaded with rocks and debris we came back to shore and burned the boat, saturated it with lake water, then covered the ashes with fresh dirt and forest vegetation. Keep in mind now, this is years before DNA was testable.

Alfie took the car to his uncle's and it was never seen again. We don't know exactly what he did with it, but Alfie told him he was in trouble and to get rid of it. We made an oath never to speak of her and we never got the chance, really. Poor Alfie took sick not long after and died not long after from acute myeloid leukemia. He was the sweetest boy and it took a lot out of me.

Sometimes he visits my dreams. He sits in that rowboat, not uttering a word, only staring at me as I repeat hush, hush. Only his presence is tangible.

The blue dress. I had bought it for the graduation prom. I imagine girls still do those things. Who knows, I'm never around young 'uns. I felt good in that rig and had searched for weeks looking for the perfect gown. And wouldn't you know it— Ophelia turned up in the very same. Only our corsages were unique. Anyway, most of us partied too much and ended up spewing our din-dins over our pretty steamed frocks. I left the prom early with someone other than my date, stepping out into that summer evening. I didn't want to be anywhere near her.

There we are on the ice. We skated on the small cove that froze over each season for winter fun. And even though we were just little bits far from the eyes of adults, we jumped on the broken ice sheets that shattered with the tides. Leaping from one floating block of ice to another. Sometimes getting wet toes from losing a foothold. That's Ana, Cindy, Liz and me all sporting pink little cheeks with wool hats and mittens. I'm holding a big stick. I'm holding on to this one.

Another family photograph: my aunt Jane and her boyfriend Dean. He was a true creep always inviting me to sit on his lap or go for a little walk far from the eyes of others. I never did. I remember his sinister eyes and his slanted grin. Why she stayed with him I'll never know. Anyhow they've all long checked out. Arriverderci.

Ophelia's family put up a big reward. The search went on for a few years with the flyers dwindling over time until the case was cold. Frosty as her heart. Folk used to say how sad it was and all that rigmarole just to sound sympathetic and to feel better about themselves, still beforehand they always said what a little bitch she was. And truth be told, she wasn't missed.

There we are at the folk festival down in the valley. Don't know half the folk in this picture. We camped there for the weekend, our own little Woodstock. We weren't yet eighteen, but we got the go ahead to hang there for the weekend. Only if our parents had known the goings-on, there would have been another story. My friend's cousin gave me some kind of tranquilizer and I missed the entire festival sleeping the day away. What a waste of time.

Here's one of mom and dad. Often it pains me to look at these images. Lost loves and dead friends. When my parents died I couldn't look at their photographs for many years. I felt their disappointment and judgements. I wasn't the easiest of daughters. I was wild, yet most of us were back then. We wanted excitement and change and we were certain that we were going to get it.

The years settle in and before you know it many have passed, accumulating alongside them age and hardships. Bitterness and banality. I know it isn't so for all folk, but it has been for me. Life is closing in. Becoming smaller and smaller and insignificant.

When I ponder at some of these frames it ignites a sort of joy or at the very least a warmth in my heart. Especially when I see the old black and whites. We all shot with black and white film back then and developed the negatives in our art school lab. We tried to be avant-garde and were for the most part. There's Erik with his blue comic book hair standing on end with spikes that nearly reached the heavens and Freda with a thousand ear studs and a nose ring. We always got into the clubs. Never had to wait in line for even a minute, anointed with the outstretched arm and pointed finger. Bloody hell, now I'm lucky if someone offers me a seat on the bus or holds a door. Societies run on their inner egos.

Lookie here. Sarah. Now Sarah was a character. Sweet name, but she could drop you in a second if you glanced sideways at her. Heard she was a veterinarian. Out in the boonies. Treating cattle and horses. Pigs and sheep. I have no use for this memento.

Man, I can't believe I've held on to this. Freddy. He raped me. I guess it's what you'd call date rape. I reckon it happened to many a girl back in the day. Everyone high on something with order unpredictable like a shifty foundation. Don't know what became of him. Bye bye.

Bryan. Now he was something or rather still is. Here he is with his face airbrushed robin egg blue. He's still around. An artist. I check him out now and again. Follow his work and installations. He has a big life. And I'm a bit jealous I must admit. I wonder if he's happy...? Folk like to pretend they are even if it isn't true. Obscuring authenticity and hiding their disappointments like an old dirty hankie.

I've taken to drink over the years. It keeps Ophelia away, off in the distance of time and space. I won't keep her photo. She's branded in my memory. A loathsome little image that I can't get rid of. Some of us have talents for obliterating recollections. But her, she's always there, like an itchy scar.

She came to me in a dream last night. Sitting in the very same rowboat with Alfie. She was talking aggressively, yet I couldn't decipher a single word. Her mouth twisted and moved and I knew she was oozing obnoxious remarks. I wanted the boat to sink, but it sat there fixed in the clear water.

Then in an instant, it drifted far out into the blue and I couldn't see their faces or imagine her words spun of scorn and spite. A dense mist descended obscuring them from sight. I hope she stays there in the fog of my mind. Never materializing as the succubus she truly was if only for a second. Let her suspend in forgotten remembrances. A mere daydream in the tempo of my camera-eye.

Bad Vibes Bob

It's difficult to say when it started. Well… not exactly. I began to notice him around the time of my bicycle accident. Some idiot was talking on her phone, opened the car door without a glance and sent me flying past the length of the hood crashing onto the street. Leaving me with a broken leg and shattered arm, plus a dismembered bike. And let's face it—I'm no spring chicken.

Furthermore, the bitch took off without offering a dram of assistance. I lay there in utter pain until some random Samaritan called for an ambulance. Oh yeah—one of my front teeth is missing.

He recently moved in across the street from me and our windows face each other. I know his name is Bob because I was standing on my balcony one day and one of the neighbours said 'hey Bob' as he was approaching his building. He appears to be a mess. Walks with a limp and is grossly overweight. It's not his girth that I find offensive. It's his atmosphere. As if he doesn't care. As if he's given up. I've never been close to him, but truthfully I feel as if he oozes body odour. His clothes never look washed and his oily hair sticks to his head like a helmet. It would be no surprise to me if blossoms wither up and die upon his approach.

It's difficult living on this third floor walk-up and I can't get any money for takeout tips. I have a thing for Thai and unbeknownst to me, on my second order, the delivery dude had taken to groping himself and rubbing his dirty hand all over my order before leaving his vehicle and walking up three flights to ring my bell. I had lost my wallet in the accident and consequently have no debit or credit cards. A merciful friend lent me a limited quantity of cash. So even though I'm a generous tipper, this courtesy could not be extended with my meagre stash. My fate was sealed when I opened the door and didn't hand over a tip, but instead awarded a toothless smile.

Upon settling down for my Asian delight I noticed strange repetitive movements in Bob's living room. There is light flickering from a large screen and just as I navigate a grilled shrimp to my lips, I hesitate just before the chopsticks graze my open mouth. He appears to be rubbing some sort of cream over his abundant mass. I have an old pair of binoculars from my bird watching days and sneak a gander from the corner of my double panes.

It isn't a lotion, but a large block of Lactantia. The weather is extremely humid of late and the butter is dripping down the valleys, gorges, and mountains of his swollen frame. He is flapping his arms like some grounded bird begging for take-off. This act seems off-colour and odd to say the least; still I'm compelled to examine him, and as I do, my tasty Pad Thai forfeits its heat. I enjoy my food scalding hot, nevertheless I try to imagine what he is intending. Is it an action to hydrate the skin or something sexual? Perhaps prep for a Tinder date?

Taking a break from Bob, I sit down to serious television, but there isn't anything of interest to watch despite the telecommunications company extorting considerably for these chosen stations. Incidental thoughts are dispersed as I suddenly remember a disturbing reoccurring dream. I'm lying in bed with a famous older actor and he's trying to enter me from behind. His member is like a folded elephant trunk and I keep repeating, "give it up, I'm not into that". I don't want to think about it anymore, yet each night he returns. What's up with that?

Being cooped up is taxing. My upstairs neighbour is a pathological pacer traipsing to and fro as if the devil's breath is hot upon her neck. The floors creak and rest is but a distant wish. I dream of throwing her off the balcony, seeing her tight little grimace staring off to some unchartered sphere. Yet, I'm only able to whack the ceiling with my crutch when it becomes all too consuming. Thus, Bob has become my distraction. The lone vulture on the tree. Live theatre so near. Nonetheless, how to decipher his behaviour?

I've taken a break from Thai and switched to Italian. The delivery guy had become steadfastly chilly. I know it's the tips. Or should I say... lack of.

But little did I know after the second order of Linguine with Lemon the delivery guy had taken to spitting in my order like the scene from Casino when Nicky's brother Dominick hacks in the takeout for the Los Vegas cops.

One of those actors is in my sex dream, but I'll keep that to myself.

It's spring and the leaves from the giant Linden tree outside my balcony separating Bob's windows from mine have not quite emerged. Bob and I are among the folk who boldly leave our fenestellas bare. Void of curtain or cloak. It isn't as if I'm prancing around naked for all the street to see. However, sometimes I run down my hall and through the dining room naked as a jaybird when I forget some item after a bath. And if someone were to steal a peek, I can sense their shocked gaze from my jiggling junk, despite the fact they that can't steer away.

Because of my confinement and shattered limbs Bob has become my go to when the light has faded. I'm worried because each day the opening foliage tucks him further away. The sky has settled into a rich teal and the visible stars and dippers often concealed by cloud or smog, reveal themselves. It is only at this time of the evening I can observe. A woman of similar mass has joined him.

Bob is naked from the waist up and she too with the exception of her bra. They anoint themselves in butter then embrace in a waltz-like state. They shove and push each other. Their limbs scuffle and tussle like sumo wrestlers. Hands glissade down hidden ribcages and muscles buried deep within each thickened hide. It's too far away; still I can smell their sweat and perspiration. The humidex is off the charts and I can only imagine the funk that envelopes that room. It's a sight to behold all right and I'm bent on understanding this fusion. Then, all of a sudden, the lights go out all over the hood. The storm picks up and power will be out for an undetermined amount of time.

The following morning debris scatters all over the street: fallen branches and downed trees. My Linden tree is strong and upright without one lost bough, the leaves have burst into life once again and Bob is but a puzzle. Obscured until late the following autumn. I conjure up Bob most evenings, conceptualizing him with his oleo in hand. Engaging in his Sumo Rama dance. His place in the story of life.

A Weed in the Canyon

Clementine just purchased a small two-storey house on Willow Glen Rd in Laurel Canyon with a lush side garden teeming with lemon, lime and orange trees. It's absolutely lovely and completely renovated. She scrimped and saved her entire life and, with the help of an inheritance from an uncle, purchased it for one buck shy of a million, which is a steal for this area. The move isn't at all practical. For one thing she isn't American and will have to leave the country every six months in order not to be labeled an illegal alien. Nonetheless, she's here.

Clementine had visited California and many of its counties numerous times wishing she could move to the Golden State. She doesn't know a soul; yet an undeniable lure has brought her here. It's the mystique of it all that played a significant slice of her decision. Much has happened here, the music scene that changed a generation, but that history is spent. Even so, there is an aura about this place. Maybe it's only the warmer weather. It certainly puts a smile on a face instead of freezing one's ass off as the northern neighbour where polar winds bite at a face, freeze toes and every single bone aches and cries out for comfort.

She has no clue what to expect from relocating. Change. Something. No matter how insignificant. It felt as if days have remained stagnant the last twenty years and now that's she's left the life of the worker bees, she wishes to venture somewhere unknown. Taking in the scents of all unchartered.

It's the first time in her life that she will live in a detached home since childhood. For her entire adult life she has lived in apartment buildings hearing the continuous slamming of doors. Haunted by noise and smells of cooking not to her liking. This house is open and airy with an ultra-modern kitchen, dining and living room all in one breadth. Glass pilot doors open to a patio area and upstairs there is additional living space with a fireplace for cool evenings, a closed bedroom, a courtyard off the second level and a roof garden. It's sleek and sexy. What more could she wish for?

In all her years Clementine never really learned to drive. When she was young she had been in a serious car accident and two of her cousins had died. She never got over her nervousness of vehicles even if it hasn't been constructive for her life. She does maintain a driver's license, though never drives. She forced herself to acquire one to overcome her fear. Still, she has only been behind the wheel three times in sixteen years.

Her home is situated on a bend high up in the canyon and the closest store is more than an hours' walk. Still, it will help with her weight. She has let herself go the last years. Hiding under think layers of clothes, a requirement most of the year, with only a sliver of warmer weather allotted for thinner attire. Here lifestyle is paramount. Fitness. Clean habits. She never gave up smoking. It's not a heavy addiction, nevertheless she can't say no when having a drink and this has become more of a problem of late. *Hell, can't I have something?* It's her go to for when she's overdone it.

She sold everything, keeping only a few photographs inside her three large suitcases. Got rid of all her heavy attire. A fresh start—that's what's needed. Her kin are all gone and she is child-less. What was there to keep her there—nothing. She looks at a photograph of her five-year old self, standing beside a snowman proudly pointing at her creation. It feels so different here with the ocean off in the distance and palm trees erect and alien.

There isn't a thing to eat. Only a can of espresso she brought in one of her bags. Not even a drop of milk, regardless she makes a stovetop brew. She'll need the energy to traipse down the hill to the Canyon Country Store and back up again. She grabs a few bags and begins her descent down the winding road. The heat is intense and it scorches her exposed skin. Humidity attacks her hair making her grey locks look like a deviant scrub brush. Often cars pass. Some with surfboards, yet no one offers a lift.

She's happy to be back in the land of Anglophones after leaving the French province, where she had become one of those people who swore she never would be. One that had lived there for decades, but whose French had remained shabby at best. She did try, but she was always lousy with languages and only had English acquaintances. French was not required for her job with an international import/export company and now she relishes in the thought that if she needs directions or whatever, she can easily converse in her mother tongue. Instead of doing her French best and getting a "Hein-quoi?" Which is the Québécois equivalent of "What the fuck did you say?"

She finally reaches the Canyon Country Store and flops down on the seat outside before venturing inside to purchase some provisions. They say, sometimes, you can see famous people here, although today there are only loud-mouthed, skimpily-dressed millennials wearing Lululemon and baseball caps snapping selfies.

After having a meal and buying all the food items she can easily carry, she begins her amble up the road. By the time she reaches her house she is drenched in sweat and thirsty beyond belief. How she wishes for a frosty Margarita, but she doesn't have any Tequila in the house. Beer was too heavy to lug up the hill, so she settles for a warm rosé with ice.

As Clementine sits on her garden terrace she feels a tinge of happiness. She does not believe in this state-of-mind. She simply isn't wired this way. She remembers hints of such a feeling when playing with childhood friends, having a laugh when tripping or in the first bloom of love, but not in the day-to-day and all the therapy in the world won't change that. When folks say, "I'm great" she believes they are total phonies and liars. Even so, her mood is lighter today.

The city is beautiful lying beneath her feet, especially at night when it is aglow and brimming with life. She ventured into downtown LA a few times to lunch watching the many young fit bodies strolling along the sidewalks, but felt consciously exposed in the sizzling sunlight with all of her abundance displayed in plain sight. She wished herself back up north enshrouded in heavy clothing—a tuque and winter coat and winding scarf partially concealing her face and neck. Here, there is no escaping. No snow gusts or freezing rain, or thousands of brown-red turned maple leaves encircling one's sphere.

It becomes more and more unusual for her to venture down into the city even though it awaits a few minutes from her doorstep. And although she loves the sea and went to the beach a few times, she was too scared to swim. The strong temperamental currents frightened her. She imagined them sucking her far out into the blue with hungry sharks lurking under the swell, ravenous for her generous form. She did enjoy the surfers though, admiring their courage and their highly developed art of riding the waves.

Even though it's preferable to have her food and liquor delivered from favourite downtown shops, she still sets off every other day down to the Canyon Store. One afternoon after leaving the store she is offered a lift. A yellow, vintage Volkswagen van with a white top slows down alongside her.

"Hey there, you're lugging a load. Can I offer you a ride?"

He looks friendly enough, with a smiling dog panting out the window; nevertheless he could be the local loony, but she accepts. The van grinds into gear and makes a series of wheezing sounds that reminds her of the van in *Little Miss Sunshine*, trying to stay the course with all of its troubles.

"Where ya heading?

"Willow Glen Road."

"No problem, we'll be up there in a jiff. It would be a shame to let a lady trudge up this road with all that gear you're toting."

"What's your name?"

"Clementine."

"And you?"

She somehow expected him to say Jax or Zane. Something vernacular Californian.

"I'm Bernie. And this is Chili Pepper."

"Well, this is very kind of you, Bernie."

The dog quietly wags her tail revealing patches of heavily matted fur.

When they reach her house he beams.

"Maybe we'll run into each other again."

She returns his smile watching as he turns the rig around with its groans and spurts of pain. He waves out of the side window and drives and slowly making his way down the hill. After he is out of sight, she thinks that was kinda nice. She has become somewhat fatigued with herself. Solitude has a shelf life.

When moving in, her next-door neighbours came by to welcome her and say hello, promising to invite her over once they returned, but they were heading to Sicily for five months. The only contact she has with folk here is the staff at the Canyon Store.

Clementine's used to it. She's more of a loner, although she can be quite social when she needs to be. The older she's become people have become less significant to her. She prefers the company of birds or hearing the distant barks of coyotes that howl through the canyon every evening. Often they compete with hoot owls serenading everyone within earshot.

A hummingbird feeder hangs from one of the lemon trees and sometimes the birds come close to her like tiny fairies. One morning a coyote was standing on her patio with three of her cubs. Clementine threw some sliced meat cuts, which they gobbled up like there was no tomorrow. Afterwards, she thought perhaps she had made a mistake. One shouldn't tamper with wildlife. Imagining them moving in, awaiting grub every day, yet that was their only visit.

Bernie settles in for the evening on an empty lot further down the canyon disclosing remnants of an old foundation. His van is camouflaged amongst hearty overgrowth. He knows this locale is only temporary. Soon enough, the builders will arrive to construct a new home.

He is accustomed to upheaval and has been homeless for years now. At first, he had aspirations of becoming a singer and drifted to Los Angeles in the early eighties. Initially he got gigs as backup vocals and playing acoustic guitar in clubs on the Strip, though in the end it never amounted to anything. He ended up doing odd jobs, mostly in restaurants. He gave it up completely following a motorcycle accident, which left him lame and in constant pain. Forcing him to walk with a cane carved from a tree branch.

Sometimes he busks for money downtown. The tourists are the most generous. Thinking he's some old throwback from the music scene way back when. Often he eats in soup kitchens and wanders the hills inquiring about yard work and handyman jobs that can earn him a few bucks.

Clementine's out of the loop as far as scoops go. The last time she read the news she saw a photograph of a wild elephant lying dead in a river somewhere in India. Someone had given it explosive fruit. It disgusted her and she vowed to stay clear of what's going on in the world. It's only shit.

The house is absent of a television or stereo. She wasted so much time staring at the screen and withdrew from music years ago. Compressed with neighbours and paper-thin walls. Sometimes, though, she twirls around her open space like some excited Dervish. Especially when she hears a tune from the B52's or the Ramones or something else to her liking from a car's open window. She thinks *a party would be amusing*, but there's no one to invite.

One evening while sipping a cocktail on her patio she hears a familiar sound. The voice of the van. It seems to be conking to a stop in front of her house and lets out a long series of grunts. She heads to the door and sees Bernie with a bouquet of wild-flowers. Chili Pepper sits obediently at his feet.

"Bernie. This is unexpected."

"Thought I'd take a chance."

Handing her a mix of locally grown blossoms.

"Well, come in."

She isn't at all certain why she invites him in. Though truth be told she is bored with hardly a soul to chat with and celibacy has become too close a companion.

"Would you like a cocktail?"

"That would be nice."

Clementine goes to the kitchen and Chili Pepper follows close behind. She prepares icy Margaritas in the blender and brings them out to the patio.

He sits across from her taking a deep, long swallow.

"This is really tasty."

"Want another?"

"Sure. Can't say no to that."

She produces two additional delicious dripping glasses and returns with a plate of assorted cheese, crackers, seedless grapes, and a bowl of cold water for Chili Pepper, which the dog gulps down as if it is her last moment on earth. She is offered a few bits of cheese and following her treat, gazes back at Clementine with a grateful smile.

"So, Bernie, are you still working?"

She does not find this intrusive for they are of similar age.

"I do landscaping from time to time. Keeps me active."

After the second drink Bernie asks Clementine if he can take a shower.

"I never had the chance before dropping by. I was in the neighbourhood you see."

Although she finds this odd and feels put on the spot, she agrees providing him with a fresh towel. She feels it would be unkind of her to refuse him. A considerable amount of time passes before he emerges cleaner with bits of water lingering in his full, longish hair.

There's no denying he's a good-looking man, reminiscent in a certain angle of light of a young Sam Shepard. Inviting, in a definite, raffish way.

"I feel like a new man! Thanks, I really needed that."

Bernie has started to come over more frequently, but she wonders why he never invites her out to dinner, a movie or anything for that matter. She just assumes he's stingy, an attribute she doesn't respect in a man. Still, overall she likes him. He told her about his past. How he grew up on a farm in the Midwest. How he hated it. Forced to do chores upon chores day in day out. How his mother died from an accident when he was four. How his father was mean and beat him and the minute he was old enough to leave he headed here.

By the end of the month he is practically living with her. She even buys steep-priced chow for Chili Pepper from a vet. Chili has taken a shining to Clementine and often Bernie will have to limp over just to rub her head and get a wagging tail. His pained hip doesn't hinder his sexual performance though, which has proved to be an added benefit to the friendship.

One afternoon down at the Canyon store one of the guys, Wyatt, whom she's gotten to know well, shines the spotlight on Bernie.

"Clementine. I realize this is hardly my business, however I've seen you from time to time with Bernie. You are a nice lady and I wouldn't want you to get hurt."

"What do you mean exactly?"

"Don't get me wrong. Bernie is a cool dude and all, but he's sort of a predator."

"Predator!" You mean sexually perverse?"

"No. No, not that. A player. A sort of douche. It's just that I've seen it again and again throughout the years. A single lady comes to the Canyon and he swoops in like a bird of prey. Ya know, gets chummy, and then makes his move to gain entrée so to speak. Get me? He's homeless. Bet he didn't tell you that one. He lives in his van."

As she eats her lunch on the terrace the story of him being in the area, dropping in, and the ceaseless requests to use the shower start to sink in.

A few nights after following a carefully executed meal, Clementine puts the gears to Bernie.

"So, Bernie. Why don't you ever invite me to your place? Truthfully I get fed up with all the cooking. You know I do—you once in awhile do, would be nice."

"Oh, I will. Eventually. I'm ashamed, actually. It's a mess. You know with the bum leg and all. I'm not much of a house-keeper."

"M-m-m-m. That's funny because someone told me, someone whom I trust, that you live in your van and that you make a habit of befriending single women and moving yourself in. Trust me, I hate liars and I've met plenty throughout the years."

"Man. If I had told you the truth would you have given me a second thought?"

"I dunno know. Maybe I'd feel less disappointed if you'd been upfront from the get-go. But you never gave me the chance. I don't judge most folk. Everyone has had hard times. In spite of that I'd like you to get the hell out. I'll find a way to contact you if I change my mind. I feel totally deceived and ripped off."

"Clementine, please believe this wasn't my intention. I would have told you sooner or later."

Bernie gathers up his few belongings and his guitar and calls for Chili Pepper who knows a good thing and hides herself where no one can find her.

"Chili Pepper… come on, girl. Chili…"

But before he can sniff her out Clementine pushes him out the door. Cane and all. An old tattered duffle bag just misses his head.

Several weeks have passed and no sign of Bernie. She feels bad about keeping Chili and is certain Bernie pines for his dog. Clementine puts a note on the message board of the Canyon Store alerting Bernie that Chili Pepper is happy and misses him since he doesn't answer his phone. She asks Wyatt to tell him to stop by if he runs into him, but it is as if he has dropped off the planet. Or abducted for that matter.

Truth be told, Bernie has already hooked up with another lady. A new addition to the Canyon, a newbie from London named Arabella. He left his van on the entrance driveway to the vacant lot, partially concealed by heavily laden foliage and high-tailed it down Mexico-way with his new squeeze. Not giving Clementine a second thought and a mere nano-second for Chili Pepper. Thanking his lucky stars that he didn't have to stash her somewhere while he's off gallivanting down South with Arabella, whom he met when helping her with car trouble and charmed her on the spot right then and there.

Rain has been falling heavily the last week keeping Clementine housebound, preventing her from going down to the Canyon Country Store. Instead, she watches the worrisome stream of brown earth running down the road in front of her house. Chili Pepper has never been happier since her groom and shampoo down at the doggy salon. If Bernie were to appear now she'd give him the cold stare, ignore him and exit the room retreating to one of her many hiding places.

The downpour continues without pause and unbeknownst to Clementine the earth has started to shift. First, she hears a rumbling like an oncoming train. When she looks outside she sees that part of the road has caved in and her next-door neighbours' house has collapsed like an accordion from the swiftly accelerating mudslide. She picks up Chili Pepper and speedily walks down the road stepping over fallen trees, boulders and structural debris.

After walking for some time, she sees the back of the yellow van lurking from under a palm branch. She opens the door and gently puts Chili in the back on the worn sleeping bag before rummaging around for the keys that are soon discovered taped to the roof of the glove compartment. To her amazement it starts without hesitation, although a little surly and stubborn. She turns the yellow van around, which sighs in disapproval, and heads down the Canyon with one wonky wiper clearing the way.

Finders Keepers

As a child I loved visiting his studio—a small room upstairs off my parent's bedroom. Filled with scents from paint and turpentine. Easels. Paintings, books and palettes positioned for optimum workspace. Carousels of colour spun corner to corner. Burnished leaves and trees—reflections against water. Hills, fields and faraway skies all harmonized with his gift of colour and unique brush strokes.

My father was a well-known Canadian landscape artist from Nova Scotia. He painted in oils and nearly always on panel board. Occasionally a canvas was substituted. He would have preferred to live in a cabin away from everything if he had been able to. These are his words.

"Who can deny the mood or feelings created by the glint of early morning sunshine on a patch of swamp grass, the magic of maple and poplar on an autumn hillside, the wonderment of a quiet stillwater nestled among spruce and pine, the mystery and serenity of a hardwood hill in the late afternoon of a winter's day, the breath of a spring wind crossing a lake, the smell of damp moss in the shadows of a forest swamp, the mood and power of the land and elements?"

It hit hard. I received the news via an art auctioneer twenty-three years after my parents' death by car crash. You see—the individuals that bought our family home had found two hundred paintings between the floorboards, hidden under the kitchen floor above the basement ceiling. They held on to them all that time. Withholding. Stole the inheritances from two young sisters and the rightful guardians of their father's late work. A secure retirement.

Rape. That's what if feels like. Sadness and anger are the initial responses. Vengeance follows soon after. I procured a good lawyer and paid thousands only to be told… "Finders keepers." Sometimes, intellectual law isn't very intelligent. The only thing I managed to salvage was copyright control. The collector can't reproduce any images of his sleazily acquired collection in the form of books or anything that make profit.

I was enraged by the thought that I chose to hold back the remining work from public view for twenty years, slowly releasing a few beautiful panels at a time, and now this collector was flooding the market with multiple exhibitions. Auctioning them off. Dealing with hick galleries—attempting to make a quick buck. Devaluing my father's good name. Art dealers knew how he got them, bad business to represent.

When I told the collector how much I disrespected the handling of the work, he threatened me with a lawyer. A schoolyard bully. I took action. I plotted and planned. Never confronting the thieves directly and the collector only once, but found the whereabouts of their residences, cottages, business and parking spots.

It was difficult to witness my father's paintings being represented in such cheap fashion. Pondered what recourse would prove optimally effective. Those of us who have ever lived in Halifax, know all about rats. We joke how the harbour rats are as big as cats. And they are. I researched how to trap them. Constructed a trap approximately 1-foot by 3-feet long, with support beams and plywood fastened by glue and nails.

It was a rectangular box with an opening at each end. A mesh netting supported the top and the bottom was enclosed by plywood. One end was sealed off. A thin pipe secured the prop-up door. A wire was attached to the pipe and bait, consisting of peanut butter and fish guts, was inserted. And when my dear rat gnaws at the wire… voilà! Gotcha! I made three.

Preceding this plan, I broke the same window at the collector's place of business multiple times at one-month intervals, but never the same date. I chose my moment and managed to avoid the security camera—calculating each scan of the lot. I wore varied disguises, sported gloves and carried a small rake to erase my footprints. Scratched his vehicle after each paint job. But this wasn't enough.

My parents' house passed hand a few times, but Halifax is small and I managed to track down the original buyers who hoarded my father's paintings waiting for the right buyer. They lived outside the city. The lot is well stocked with bushes and trees, thus numerous places to hide. I tested the traps with my cat Daleighla, putting Temptations and wet food inside. Each time she went for it, the trap door dropped and shut.

I drove to a secluded part of the shoreline outside the city and positioned the traps along the bank. Weighted by rocks that were laid on top. Camouflaged with seaweed and odd pieces of debris. The night was clear with little wind. The scent of the sea was lush. A calm washed over me like a warm soft wave.

People sleep better encased by cool sea air. Cozy under the blankets. I dozed off counting rats. Each one chewing wires—spawning offspring. Dancing the rooms of the intended. Dawn broke as I headed toward my traps. I bought an egg salad sandwich and café du lait in a thermos for breakfast. The rocks were slippery from dew and sea mist. Gulls greeted.

When I arrived, six little angry eyes peered. Voices squeaked. Tails twirled all about. There were a few extra slices of bread in my bag. Tossing them to the hungry beasts I contemplated… which home would I visit first? It wasn't difficult intercepting the schedules of each culprit. What time the collector crossed the bridge. When he left. What restaurants he frequented. Sunday dinners and barbecues. Visits to the in-laws. Church. Identical detective work was completed for the thieves.

I headed up the embankment with two traps, then one, placing them on the back seat of my car. We drove along the road that joins the small seaside communities with the city. Small coves and open sea beyond the harbour. I passed my old family home, the yacht club and familiar markings of childhood. Thoughts were of the dead. My parents and younger sister. The rats continued squeaking. We had a stopover at the place that I was house sitting for a week, where additional food and water was provided. They required nourishment to fulfill their missions—peanut butter and tuna. I went to the veranda, wine in hand, mentally preparing my next move. Dusk fell, swallows called in the evening sky.

The rats were kept at home for the next couple of days. My car substituted for a rental. This was mandatory. There were continual switches. Wigs, latex, gloves, bleach and various cleaning products were stored in a carpenter's box. The thieves were away for a few days, when they'd return—no idea. This was a throw of the dice. The fatter rat was allocated for them. I felt certain it was a female, her full belly brushing the bottom of the box with each turn. Hopefully a pregnant one, blessed with a generous litter.

Two of the traps were laid on the backseat. I put on Patti Smith and turned the engine. Twilight was here, the sky a dark teal blue. Stars sprouted on the horizon. I took the highway to the thieves lair. Turning onto a small, quiet road about a quarter mile from their house. The traps were awkward and heavy as I traipsed along the ditch ready to hide amongst the trees and bushes if car lights were spotted. Prickly twigs and branches edged me along.

The house was in darkness. A small exterior light was on above the front door. Clouded by flies and moths. I waited. Checking for any interior movement. It was a large secluded lot with no direct views to neighbours scattered along the country road generously distanced. I left my traps in the shrubbery and assessed entry points. The basement window was slightly ajar. It wasn't big, but had sufficient space to drop my captives. I went back to the bushes and grabbed the boxes. I wore thick work gloves. Once the traps were positioned along the basement wall, I opened the first one, then the other. Grabbed each rat by the tail and guided them through the window. My lovelies disappeared within the darkness. I'll be back.

When I arrived home, Daleighla purred and demanded pats. I secured my third rat in the basement with food and water. The door firmly closed to prevent Daleighla adding further stress to the poor confined creature. The collector had a seaside cottage. This was a weekday. Usually, he frequented it only on weekends or holidays. I had driven there several times—the last two days ago. Quiet. Only birds and sea loons welcomed me.

Upon approach the black night closed in. My rental was parked strategically off a small U-turn. I left the trap in the car and cased the place. All was as it should be, void of movement and life. There were no open windows. The entire place sealed like a tomb.

I pried open a four-season window with a heavy flat screwdriver and returned to retrieve my rat. Gently dropped it in. The collector had a speedboat docked on the shore—a Stingray 225sx. It was deep red and sleek. I added sugar to the gas tank before embarking up the hill. Another successful mission.

Heading home serenity enveloped me. Not a pang of guilt or doubt probed at my conscience. The night was clear and stars guided me along the road. A full moon lured me along. My thoughts were of my father. Fields and brooks. Red leaves against rock. Paint brushes in a jar. Felt his soft smile upon my brow.

La Chambre

In the beginning she came into the world lucky. She lived in a stately house surrounded by lush gardens and vegetable patches. There was a babbling brook that ran into a trout-filled pond and orchards of fruit dotted the land. The halls were wide and ample with high ceilings and huge square rooms. The floors were polished and gleamed richly under the lights displaying their warmth when the sun rested upon their boards.

The salon was painted crimson with warm white borders on the baseboards and mouldings. The kitchen—open and airy was painted in warm butter tones with white accents punctuated by flecks of red here and there forcing the eye to dance about the space in a delightful quickstep She did all the things fortunate girls do. Took riding lessons and ballet, even though it was hushed behind her back 'too big-boned'. She liked to observe the stars at night and dreamt of becoming one herself.

She had gone to good schools and graduated with honours in classical history even though it wasn't practical for the job market. She travelled following her studies and did an extended stretch in Italy embracing the architecture, monuments, culinary gems and men before returning home.

Her marriage followed. At first, she envisioned that she was well suited for this institution. He was dependable, considerate, but as time went on he became dull and duller. She ended up having a series of affairs and eventually left him settling on the last of these tries. Thinking him the best of the bunch.

He was exciting and a skilled lover. Carried an air of danger about him. He was all that her former husband was not. She divorced and remarried. They travelled abroad and played tennis. Lunched and dined out. Entertained. That was then.

Initially, she adored her man, yet was never really quite sure what he did for a living. Entrepreneurial, he described himself. Yes, something about hedge funds. Things she didn't have much interest in or understanding of. She put her absolute trust in him never thinking for a moment that anything was amiss.

Instead, she focussed on herself. Keeping fit and limber with yoga and massages. Biweekly facials and skin treatments. She saw this has her role. Looking the best she could, because she thought that was what he wanted. What he did want was what she came with. The property that soon would be hers since she was an only child and her one remaining parent had one foot close to the grave. It wouldn't be long for him to collect.

In the spring of that long ago year he got his wish. Her mother died and the estate passed down to her. He suggested they put the home up for sale immediately. Too much upkeep, too much to worry themselves about. And even though she had a strong sentimental attachment to her childhood home she quickly agreed. Well, for one thing was she ever going to live there again?

After the estate was settled, he had a little talk with her suggesting that the bulk of the money should be invested. He knew a good thing when he saw it. He had a feeling for business opportunities and just look at them. Until now, had he ever let them down? Without legal council and paper she agreed and permitted him to liquidate their assets into his holding company, Greenback.

In retrospect she was just plain stupid. Dumb as a post, as they sometimes say. Not one tiny space allotted for a second opinion on the matter. Their finances were wiped out two years later and he was arrested for investment fraud. A Ponzi scheme. The feds took everything. The house and what little dribblings were left in the joint bank account. There was nothing offshore. And she thought him so smart. Really. She could only stand there shocked with her mouth open not able to take in a full breath.

Within a matter of weeks she was out on the street. In time, she was cleared of any wrongdoing. Hey, wasn't she the victim in this tragedy? It took some doing to convince them of her innocence and gullibility. They just couldn't believe that a woman from means had let her crook of a husband control their assets, but, hey, they'd seen it all before. Time and time again, just another sad tale.

Throughout her marriage she was solitary. She never had any women friends. She was never what one would call a girls' girl. She was always with him. Like two peas in a pod. Now there wasn't anyone to reach out to. The first thing she did when she was released from jail was head to social services. This was advice given by her court appointed lawyer. Hell, he had even given her a few hundred bucks to help her on her way.

In the meantime she was given the address of a halfway house. The court had arranged a temporary place for her there. They just couldn't throw her out on the street. A woman alone with no means of support, they had public opinion to uphold or at the very least, an illusion of one, as this case had received a fair bit of attention in the media.

The welfare folk didn't give her a difficult time. They simply looked at the court documents and temporary housing address and filled out the applicable paperwork. They gave her a couple hundred dollars for initial emergency funding until her check would arrive at the beginning of the following month.

As she exits the office, the cold wind gnaws at her skin and bites at her bones. She does have a decent coat though. When the bailiffs came to the house they let her keep most of her clothing, except for some designer bags and all of her jewellery. She had given a large number of pieces to her housekeeper who sadly accepted with sympathy for the loss of her own job and now former employer—Isabella.

Isabella arrived at the shelter with three suitcases. One with odds and ends such as photographs and nostalgic bits and bobs that she envisions looking at wherever her feet may land. The other ladies of the shelter look at her suspiciously initially. Isabella doesn't sport the look of hardship on her face, which glows with the history of many a facial. She is lean and doesn't have a drop of fat on her toned body.

She takes her appointed place and slides her good luggage under the bed. She smiles at her roomies and one nods and the other two smile and say welcome, for who are they to judge this lady who has come so far down the rabbit hole. Isabella offers her hand and says hello, states her name and gently puts her hand back in her lap. Two ladies begin to tell their stories of woe and mistreatment by their men. Restraining orders. One is there for the booze and another for meth. Isabella feels completely separate from the ladies. Following her saga in explanation for being there, the women look at her with uncertainty. She sure ain't one of them.

Two weeks later after the uncomfortable stay at the halfway house she was given an address by the social worker. It is a small apartment building, ironically not too far from where she used to reside. The wealthiest burrow in the city. The turn of the century building consists of many one-room apartments. She is shown a ground floor unit, which faces the street and fortunately has a large bay window that lets ample light in. The floors are wood, but worn and scuffed. They creak when walked upon and she can hear the neighbour's radio upstairs blaring some francophone talk show.

The landlord is matter of fact and hands over the keys. Not at all interested in Isabella's situation or past. Rent is due at the first of each month. She doesn't know how she will make it as her social assistance barely covers expenses. Thankfully, utilities are included and it's furnished, but hideously with items from the thrift store or found items from the street. She lets out a mournful sigh and sits on the plastic chair.

The room has an odd odour. Like someone had lived here a thousand years and never once opened the window. The first thing she does is pry the stubborn pane free and let the air circulate to take out what leftover essence is lingering still. Yet, she fears it may have seeped into the walls itself. She opens her suitcases and begins hanging her clothes in the tiny closet. There are only about ten twisted hangers so she'll have to hit the dollar store to get some more.

And that she does. She buys some air fresheners, a few cheap edibles and some white sheets. Then set to removing all the strange patterns and colours in the room that she possibly could calming the space with alabaster neutrality. It feels quieter now. Perhaps a place to grab a thought.

She strategically places her few mementos throughout the room and a photograph of herself on her pony at her childhood home. She looks elated in the picture standing beside Harlequin, her palomino. His golden mane blowing in the wind. How innocent she looks. Completely unaware of what menace lays ahead. Penniless and nearing retirement age.

She tries to relax in the tight space. The walls seem to press closer to her. Footsteps and coughs can be heard in the room next to hers and the radio blares from above. She begins taking walks after walks to escape her small world. Every so often social services inquires about her job search, but Isabella never held down a job even though she's close to retirement age. She considers applying at her old neighbourhood grocery store, but she is scared she will encounter people she knows. Still, something has to change. She can't live on the handout. It just isn't enough. She wonders how generations of individuals survive on such a lousy pittance.

The following day at the laundromat she sees an advertisement posted for a cleaner. It's in her old hood and thankfully she doesn't know anyone at this address. She uses the public phone on the street, surprised that it still functions. For her cellphone was stolen at the halfway house and currently she does not have the funds to replace it.

She meets with the owner the following morning. Isabella offers her best smile and puts on the charm. The homeowner finds it strange that this lady who appears well-bred wants to clean her house, yet who is she to judge and she is in need of someone. It takes all kinds as they say. Isabella says she's a poet and enjoys the manual labour to rest her overworked mind.

Isabella begins the very next day and takes in the home. Wandering throughout its vast expanse. She picks up some furniture polish and applies it to the engraved banister one stroke at a time, although her attention is drawn to the floor below. The sun washes over the wooden floorboards and the grain seems alive, gleaming so bright it almost hurts her eyes. Yet, Isabella finds comfort here, as it reminds her of her lost childhood home.

Final Sentence

He sat before the notary's desk waiting to hear the coveted words.

"The bulk of the estate goes to... 'Save The Friends of the Forest', an organization your mother held dear."

"What. You've got to be kidding. Let me see that document."

"I realize this is a disappointment. A shock, in fact, but this was what your mother wanted."

"Is it now? That bitch!"

"Logan, she has left you something,"

"Oh yeah, now what would that be now? Bills—debt?"

"She left you the car. The Lexus. That's worth something."

"If she was still here, I'd tell her to shove it up her ass."

Logan got up from the richly grained table and marched out of the notary's office. He left the keys to the vehicle on the desk. He had always had a complicated relationship with his mother. She believed him to be lazy and without ambition.

"Logan, when will you get your head out of the clouds? I don't plan on supporting you forever."

He strove to be a writer and had published a fair number of short stories, but beyond that his success had ebbed. He never completed a collection. Or started a novel. He had lost his mojo of late and floundered between prolonged states of negativity and fleeting moments of hopefulness. The second, however, was not sustainable. Sending him into states of despair. His mother, Charlotte, was a high achiever and his listlessness and indirection was something that drove her to her limits.

She had always helped with his rent and living expenses. Would he ever get it together? He thought his mother cold and not maternal. A woman who never should have had a child. How come she couldn't love him for who he was? After all, she was his mother.

Charlotte hadn't been sick. In fact, she was planning a Safari the next month. She simply never woke up one morning. She had a lucky gentle exit into the unknown. He certainly never wished her any pain, but he thought to himself. Well imagine. Wouldn't you know it—easyville.

He was sad though. Not without feeling. Charlotte had been his mother. Pissed too, that she left him without security. No early retirement for him. He was sorry for all the things he wouldn't be able to say to her. And things he would have liked her to be proud of.

"Look, Mom, I've won a literary prize."

"That's lovely, Logan. I always knew you'd do it."

But that was all gone and all he was left with was regret and guilt. Oh yeah—bitterness.

Charlotte had done well for herself. She was a judge and looked at things, including him in an analytical way. The house wasn't any shack either. All paid up, big and roomy on a nice street filled with mature trees. He didn't have any nostalgia for it. But, it sure as hell was worth a bit of coin.

He preferred industrial, minimalist and modern. However, that style was far from his reach now. Did she want him to suffer? The notary had called him a few times and said that he had forgotten the car keys and also that Charlotte had left him a letter.

"My dearest Logan. I know you must hate me, but I've done this out of love. You will not find your way if everything is handed to you easily like a piece of bread to a duck. You are a good man. I know you will become the man you need to be, but only if the journey to your destination isn't an easy path."

He read the letter once. It was what it was. The first thing he did was sell the Lexus at a dealership. He didn't even bother to pack up the house and left the details for the notary to handle.

He was out. Isn't that what she wanted? He took a few framed photographs and firmly shut the door.

He sat in his apartment with its back alley view feeling trapped and boiling with anger. The sale from the car would only go so far. He had never held down a long-term job. He had flitted from bar to bar, restaurant to restaurant for sporadic spurts of time, never lasting for long. Charlotte always ended up bailing him out when the rent was overdue.

"When will you learn, Logan?"

He did learn that his mother never believed in him. Preferring to give her estate to some forest protection organization instead of protecting him—her one and only. She must have known how this would affect him.

Logan sees his life drawn out. Scrimping from paycheque to paycheque. Becoming one of those people who must work until they drop. No retirement for him. Well, then again, maybe he'll write that book and make a name for himself. He can just imagine Charlotte banging that hardwood gavel from the great beyond, "See, Logan, I always knew you could do it."

Hell, who is he kidding? He might as well do himself in. That would be the easiest. No, he'll take his chances at the Casino. Logan had always fought his gambling yearnings. And he had gotten into trouble on more than one occasion. Once or twice owing a loan shark. Charlotte had even been aware of the creep, yet he had never graced her courthouse. "Logan, when will you learn?"

Charlotte had tried unsuccessfully to get him to complete his addiction therapy. Yet, he only went to the therapist a handful of times. He made cheap jokes like "maybe I should try my luck elsewhere—ha ha" when they were at a standoff in the middle of a session.

Now he was taking his car-selling earnings and heading for the Casino to first to play the slots and then sit at the table of his favourite game—Pai Gow Poker. He'd even won big a few times with that one, although most of the time he lost and fell into the welcoming hands of the moneylenders.

He sat at the slots and listened to the cadence of sounds. Rhythmic and ordered. He concentrated on the icons inserting one coin after another in the machine, but alas, not a win in sight. A waitress brought him his drink and he told her to serve it at the poker table. A seat had just opened up at the table for six.

The dealer divvies out the cards, one 5-card hand and one 2-card hand for Logan as well as himself. Logan loses on the first round and wins on the second. On the third round he feels that Lady Luck is smiling on him. Nudging him to place his remaining money on this bet. "Go on, don't be a scaredy-cat. You've done it all before. You never know, do you?"

And he does. Placing the entire amount from the Lexus sell on the table. He sweats and calls out silently to anyone in the universe. "Come on. Help me a little now." Yet, he loses and downs his woes away one drink at a time.

By the time he looks at his watch the entire afternoon and most of the evening have passed in a blur. Now he's wiped out with only a few dollars left in his bank account and that familiar tune of 'why don't you end it all' starts to ring in his ears.

Just as he makes his shaky walk to the door his old friend taps his shoulder. "Now, now, Logan. Are you planning to give up? Why not give it another go? You know I'll stake you." Logan sits at the table again. Hand after hand greedily taking his coin. The dealer attempts to look compassionate all the while a tight little grin lies unhidden on his face.

Then Logan brightens up. As if an explosion of optimism explodes in his head. He sees it all now. A passage. A template for his book:

Character, handsome and talented with a weakness for gambling finds himself within the clutches of loan sharks. He is clever, however, and finds a way to outwit the crooks he owes money to by disguising himself and running off on the high seas. He becomes a merchant mariner. Lives in foreign lands. Has a lady in every port. Never heard of again…

AND THEN

"*And then?* That was the singular question in the suicide note. What could Hugo have meant? He had been fortunate, while in this world, cultivating a rather distinguished career as an architect. This allowed him to acquire a broad-based investment portfolio that made him feel secure negotiating the precarious paths of the world. Money mattered to him. He was accomplished. Our relationship had its ebbs and flows, but then what couple's doesn't? I suppose he felt life had become mundane, and then or what now had become a constant ponder. Perhaps he wanted to find out if there was a then or a now. Yet he wasn't a religious man. Not in any sense. An atheist in fact. Nor did we ever discuss such things. OK, maybe in the beginning, when we first met and were just discovering one another. Still, we never belonged to any organized theological club."

"You never told us how he did it, Augusta."

"He died of an overdose. Hoarded his painkillers over the years, unbeknownst to me. Even though he remained extremely active, lean and youthful looking with a full head of generous locks, he'd had a series of closely linked surgeries including two knee replacements, one hip replacement, plus a fractured leg and arm from a bicycle accident. I had no clue he had been contemplating this. He kept his thoughts close to his chest. What do you make of that?"

"I don't know, Augusta. Maybe we never really know one another."

"But I've known you two for decades, as long as Hugo. We don't have any secrets. Do we?"

Augusta looked at both Frankie and Lola, her two oldest friends. But neither answered, only sighed in unison.

"What am I going to do with this house? It feels so big now."

"Don't make any decisions for a while. Let the dust settle. It will take time. Now it's like the earth has been churned by a great storm."

Augusta arranged catering for the first three days. She wanted to go from A to B with barely a snag and was too distracted to focus on food and menu executions, even though she is a tremendous cook. Her friends had given up their busy schedules to be with her and she wanted them to feel comfortable despite the strained atmosphere.

The first day the house had been filled with people. Mostly close acquaintances and colleagues giving support and condolences. Thankfully, both of Hugo's parents had died. He had been an only child and she and Hugo were childless.

Augusta was pregnant when she married Hugo and they were elated about the coming child. However, the boy had been stillborn, something she never really got over. They never found the cause. Even the autopsy was inconclusive.

She assumed it was fright that killed the baby. Just before the delivery date her friend had hit a child that slid into their car on a toboggan during a snowstorm. Luckily, because of the tempest, they had been driving at a snail's pace. The kid was fine. Still, she had felt a strange sensation on impact. A sort of whoosh. Augusta knew the shock had been responsible for his death and she had never been able to have another child. Now this loss was a thing that she carried it in her pocket like a sentimental gift from a long ago hurt.

The home is minimalist in style, warmed by pieces of art and textiles such as imported rugs and wall sculpture hangings. The back of the house faces a large open garden bordered by mature gardens. An abstract birdbath fountain offers a refuge for the weary and thirsty. A lovely microhabitat support. Hugo loved watching the birds and fed them throughout the year. They got so used to him that they would often perch on his shoulders or take seeds from his open hand.

"So why do you think he did it?"

"Who knows? Maybe he was simply bored. Life can get ho-hum at times. Don't think I haven't thought about it."

"What about you, Lola?"

"Well, I have Damian. That doesn't give me the right to flirt with such thoughts."

"If you didn't have him—would this ever grace your reflections?"

"For the most part I enjoy my life. My art is going well. You know, Hugo often referred me to clients for commissions and a lot of them have panned out. I've had several successful exhibitions and my paintings are selling regularly. I feel like I have something to contribute."

Lola had hightailed to New York upon graduation. She had found a place in the East Village and had acquired a shared studio. She gained some attention, making a name for herself in the nineties. Her work is figurative, leaning towards the abstract. Painting over existing images such as photographs or prints. Reminiscent of mixed media collages. Altering the likenesses to create refitted contexts.

This manipulation of the human form generated a lot of sales at one point and life seemed easier back then. She managed to stay in New York and obtain a Green Card by paying a fellow struggling artist a couple thousand dollars to marry her for papers. And although this was decades ago, now sitting before her two oldest friends time appeared static.

The three of them had been steadily drinking and on the third night into the stay, bottle after bottle of wine finished to the end, Augusta begins to cry and is inconsolable.

"Can't believe he kept this secret from me. You think you know someone."

"Come on now, we all have our unseen and unspoken truths. For one thing, I kept my sexual orientation hidden from my family for such a long time."

"Frankie, that's not such a big deal. Your parents were so straight. Just imagine their response if you bought some swishy queen home? Or a big fur ball, for that matter."

"I have kept an incident to myself, one that I've never confessed, even to my closest lovers—a lot of them queens and fur balls. Do you remember the summer of eighty-four."

"Depends. Many things are a blur. May require a hint or two."

Both Augusta and Lola nod their heads in agreement.

"Remember the night we had a drinking contest and each of us drank multitudes of Happy Hour two-for-one Black Russians at that weird hotel we went to the one and only time."

"Yes, Frankie. How could we forget that one?"

"Augusta. You gave up soon after to go and meet Hugo, who had just finished an important school project. However, Lola and I continued on until they cut us off and kicked us out. We stumbled down to the harbour. At one point I rolled down the hill as if I was a barrel. We ended up throwing a couple of benches into the water and watched them float away wishing it were us. Don't know why we did such a fool thing. Boredom and drink can drive a soul mad. You know, Augusta, you and Hugo seemed the most content of us. But, now I've lost track of my story... Oh yeah, a while later in the evening after Lola went home, I had to move my car, which was parked in a temporary spot on the street or else I'd get a ticket. I was loaded, but certain I could manage. When I backed out, I hit a woman who was crossing the street. Ok, she wasn't where she should have been— she was literally in the middle of the street—however, I took flight and didn't stop. Just left her lying there. I was just starting law school. I would have been fucked!"

"Shit, Frankie, do you know what happened to her?"

"I heard she survived with some memory loss and a permanently lame leg. I always feel remorseful. There's never a day that passes that I don't think of her, and I've never gotten behind the wheel with even a sip of alcohol in my system since. Why do you think I give so much to MADD? For the good of my health? It's the guilt."

After completing law school, Frankie had settled in Toronto where the job market was more prevalent. Hugo and Augusta stayed in Halifax. Hugo always thought he could spruce up the skyline of the city. His structures could balance out the mish mash of the somewhat modern, Georgian and Scottish influences. However, there was always an annoying bylaw or petition prohibiting his designs and most of the time they remained unbuilt. Mere blueprints on the drawing board.

Augusta was quieter. Her crying had stopped and she was caught in a loop of continuous snivelling. Her face looked drawn and distorted.

"Let's get you to bed, Augusta. We'll be following soon after."

But they don't follow and continue to drink until the two of them become messy nearly melting into each other.

"Frankie, I too must confess something. Damian is Hugo's."

"What do you mean?"

"I mean Hugo was Damian's father."

"*No…* Who knows?"

"No one. Not even Damian."

"He's never asked?"

"Once or twice when he was young, but not since. I made up a tale. He's always been satisfied with me being his one and only. He's not interested where his other DNA provider roosted."

"Do you think that's fair for him, and for Hugo for that matter? You never gave them an option."

"Hit and run. Wow. Which one of us is worse?"

They remove themselves from the living room and stumble upstairs to bed. They're all extremely hung over in the morning, each one reaching simultaneously for coffee and a freshly squeezed orange juice.

"It's fair to say we can't shake this behaviour off like we used to."

"Certainly not."

Augusta begins rummaging in the fridge, hauling out a tray of eggs, cheese and green onions.

"Who wants bacon?"

Frankie and Lola both raise their hands as if sitting in a classroom.

"Crispy, right?"

Frankie and Lola both smile at Augusta.

"You should really let us prepare you breakfast."

"No need. I need to keep busy or I may just lose my mind."

Conversation is limited as if they're all talked out. Frankie is the first to announce his impending departure. Stating that he has to prepare for an important case he is working on, yet doesn't go into the details. Lola and Augusta have never been into law or politics so don't bother quizzing him. For Frankie it would have been a welcome distraction from the melancholy hanging around the home like a wave of high humidity.

Lola kindly decides to stay on a few more days, but Frankie leaves on an early evening flight. He insisted on taking a taxi even though Augusta said the drive to the airport would do her some good. Both are sad to see him go and hug him firmly as if a high wind would snatch him from their embrace at any moment.

"I'll call you when I get home. Love you both."

They watch as he becomes a speck on the road and disappears from view.

"Well, Lola my lovely, what shall we do with ourselves?"

They open more wine and sit down. Lola worries about her confession to Frankie. Is it safe? It better be, for she now knows a thing or two about him, not that she'd ever use it against him. What would be the point?

She feels sorry sitting before Augusta, now a grieving, childless widow. Still, what would come of it if she reveals her secret? Would it be a comfort to know a little part of Hugo lingers on? Hugo often commented on how he thought Damian resembled him in ways. Lola always brushed it off.

"Who knows who his father is? As you know I was a practicing tart and there are countless possibilities. Be certain it isn't you and the rest of them were unsuited for parenthood. No further investigation required. I never wanted the bother of dealing with the dad. No, I was always better solo."

Hugo never believed Lola and had recently filched Damian's toothbrush on his last visit and had it tested. Sure enough, Damian was his. He was furious with Lola for concealing this from him. All the wasted years. All the time he could have spent with him. Christmas and summer holidays. He would have sparked his interest in model building. Just like the ones in his studio. Damian was always excited to see what Hugo was working on whenever he came to visit. He remembered how when Damian was young how much delight he took in his model buildings, homes, tiny humans, cars and trees encompassing the interiors and exteriors to demonstrate scale. He had stewed and brewed over it. He may have even left Augusta. The fact that they weren't able to have more children had created finality. A sort of roadblock.

He also discovered that Augusta had been milking one of their savings accounts. She had given more than sixty thousand to some woman whom he had never met or even heard of. Some Lily Munchausen. Imagine! Even her family name is questionable. This Lily Munchausen had met Augusta at a café and they got to talking and repeatedly meeting up. Lily had pulled at Augusta's heartstrings by spinning a sad tale about being a single mother whose ex had hightailed it after her third child. Lily had produced three kids. The youngest some smiling, pink-cheeked cherub.

The three offspring were on loan from her cousin, Millie Fairfield. The two of them were a pair of grifters who moved around a lot trying to squeeze money from kind, gullible folk. His Augusta had proved to be one of them. Augusta, whom he had always thought intelligent and cautious had turned out to be an entirely different entity.

"You know, Lola, I just wanted to help someone and this little family seemed like such a good fit. They were desperate, as far as I thought."

"For sure Hugo would be upset. That was a hunk of change you gave away. Even if you had discussed it with him and framed them as a needy charity, I mean, you couldn't get a tax credit. What were you thinking?"

"I feel lousy enough. You don't have to rub it in. Maybe that was the tipping point for Hugo. Sent him right over the edge. And I could be the cause of it."

"Come on, Augusta. I can't imagine Hugo would have done himself in for sixty thousand."

"I dunno know. I guess."

"I mean… you and Hugo must be pretty well fixed I would imagine."

"We are. Were. What am I going to do, Lola?"

"I know you're suffering and I certainly don't want to add on, but I have something serious to discuss with you."

"Go ahead."

"A long time ago, and I mean a very long time ago, I had an affair with Hugo. Damian is Hugo's son."

"What? What did you just say?"

"I think you heard me. Damian is Hugo's son."

"How could you, Lola? All these years… all this fucking time and you kept this to yourself. You are one selfish bitch."

"I'll take that, but Augusta I felt like I was doing you both a favour. I didn't want to upset the applecart. What good would it have done? You'd hate me."

"I hate you now."

"Come on. I know you're in a lot of pain now, but we go back so long."

"If you were my friend how could you have done this to me?"

"It takes two, don't forget."

"You must have put some spell on him. Then again, he always had a soft spot for you. All of your lovers and you had to sleep with him. For that matter how can you be sure Damian is his?"

"Truthfully, I wasn't absolutely certain, even though I had a good hunch."

"You must be the cause of his death. You didn't even have the decency to let us be part of Damian's life. I bet you slept with him when we were studying together. Do you have to put your greedy mitts on everything and everyone? Did you ever consider me for one minute?"

"Sure I did. I felt like shit afterwards. No offence, but I was never interested in Hugo that way. He just was in New York at a bad junction in my life. Remember that Argentinian sculptor Rodolfo? Our torrid romance? Well, we just clicked. I never had, or will have again, such a hit off a man. We met at a group show. I had a couple of pieces in the exhibition and he came to see one of the other artists who had an instillation. I fell for him and seriously considered packing up and heading out to Los Angeles to be near him. Just as I was finalizing all the details, he simply said not to bother. The timing was off. No further explanation. I was in a state and between IUD's. Rodolfo—he was the one. My heart was fractured. That's all. I was truly broken. I thought about killing myself. Hugo comforted me. He was just there."

"Yeah, Lola. He did just that. Didn't he."

"Do you want me to leave?"

"Really, I don't know what I want, but yes I think it's best."

Damian grew up loving nature even though he never really experienced much living in New York. Sure, on summer vacation. Sometimes to Nova Scotia and Maine. One time on a road trip down the California coast with Lola and a lover of hers at the time.

He was a good student and excelled in sciences. When he was a youngster he fell in love with Bagheera, the black panther in *The Jungle Book*. And from that moment onward he decided he would study big cats, primarily the North American mountain lion and the South American black jaguar. He is just about to wind up his master's in biology in Halifax. Following this degree he plans do zoology graduate studies in England and then he will apply for a volunteer abroad program in South Africa.

He sees his entire life mapped out living the swashbuckling lifestyle of an adventurer studying these feline beasts, as well as saving them in their increasingly endangered habitats. The world has become at war with itself. Damian envisions himself as their protector.

Lola had only seen Damian briefly during her stay with Augusta. He had come to the house with a sympathy card and flowers. Augusta had hugged him deeply and was touched by his selection of blooms and for the simple fact that he had come at all. He could have waited until Lola was free before flying back to New York. Following Lola's departure, Damian's face was something she could not shake from her thoughts.

Augusta sat in her quiet home with its familiar scents. The oils on the wood, cedar in the wardrobes. She took a long breath following the absence of her guests. Augusta mulls about her life as she sits in the silent home. She had studied nutrition, yet never ended up working in her field. She couldn't find a job in the local hospitals as positions were few and far between and most people kept a tight grip on them until retirement.

She ended up being a housewife. A role she took pride in. Honing her cooking and baking skills. Taking up quilting and becoming somewhat of a local celebrity amongst the other quilters. She wishes to know Damian better and decides to make him a quilt, something of her.

He had visited on several occasions. Once for Thanksgiving dinner, and for random Sunday invites. Damian doesn't know Augusta well. He had known Hugo better and his death had saddened him. When he did come for dinners he recalled Augusta had made an effort to ask him about his interests and future plans. What little he knew of her he liked. She seemed kind.

Augusta is known for her abstract quilts. In fact, she has a large studio in the back of the house equipped with a longarm quilting machine. She begins Damian's quilt, a simple design and makes a silhouette of a black panther against a batch of deep blues, which represent a waterfall. A moody medley of greens forms the borders. She has worked feverishly on it since Lola's departure and it has been helpful, keeping her mind from dwelling on Hugo for a rare moment or two. Lola has called repeatedly, but Augusta hasn't answered her calls or texts. Frankie had reached out too and she informed him that she was coping and persevering.

Augusta managed to find out where Damian lives. She found a piece of paper in Lola's room with his address and a long list of grocery items: filet mignon, shrimp, haddock filets and lots more. She guesses since Mommy had been in town, she had stocked him up with all of his favourite goodies. Now it is her turn to give him something. She has put a great deal of effort into this quilt and hopes he will cherish it and bind himself a little to her.

Damian lives alone in a typical downtown flat in an older two-storey house. Damian's apartment is on the top floor and has a private balcony, which he has strung with multi-coloured Tibetan prayer flags. Augusta takes a chance and plans to surprise him. Hoping to catch him at home at suppertime. Perhaps he is preparing his evening meal. Some exotic feast made from Lola's extravagant edibles.

She walks up to the front door and rings the bell. She rings it three times before heading down the flight of stairs leading to the sidewalk. Then she hears.

"Hello there. Can I help you?"

"Damian. Hello. It's Augusta."

"Oh… Augusta. What a surprise."

Damian stands in the doorframe rubbing a towel through his wet hair.

"Sorry I made you wait. I just got out of the shower. Come in."

"Thanks. I know you are a student of big cats and I needed something to keep me busy after Hugo's… well you know."

"Yes. Again, I'm so sorry."

"Anyways, I made this for you. Good for the damp winter nights."

"Thank you. Would you like a coffee? I'm just about to make a new pot."

"Sure, that sounds nice."

Damian unwraps the sky-blue tissue paper and it slowly drifts like a leaf to the scuffed hardwood floorboards.

"Wow, Augusta. It's beautiful! Thanks a bunch."

A smile ignites his handsome face. After examining it, he gently folds and places it onto the back of one of the kitchen chairs.

"It must have taken you a lot of time. It's so detailed."

"Like I said, it kept me busy. So when will you be finished your studies here?"

"In just over two months. Can't believe how fast it's gone. I've enjoyed it here, but am more than ready to start my next thing."

"London, right? I heard a doctorate in zoology."

"Yup. Really looking forward to it. I've heard nothing but good things about the program."

As she sits, she searches for resemblances of Hugo. There is a likeness across the eyes and the shape of his nose. Yes she can see him there. Though his mouth is full and sensual like Lola's, his eyes are green like Hugo's.

"Augusta, milk and sugar?"

"Please."

They drink their coffee in awkward silence. Following the second cup of coffee, Damian rises and says, "Well, I better get back to my studies. Have several essays to complete. Got to crack on with the assignments."

"Of course."

Augusta gets up and heads to the door.

"Till later then. Take care."

Although touched by Augusta's gift, he feels it is an odd gesture. All of the effort involved in such a creative endeavour to give it away to someone she really doesn't know. He wraps the quilt around himself as he sits before his computer carelessly spilling several drops of coffee on the pristine cotton without a second's notice.

"That was nice of her. I have it wrapped around me now. I must admit it's really comfy, Mom. I'll take a photograph of it and send it to you."

He spreads the quilt over the cream-coloured sofa and takes a full-on shot.

"Yes, it's really lovely. It must have taken her a quite a considerable investment of time. That's probably why I haven't been able to reach her."

"I know, Mom. She told me that she needed the diversion from Hugo's death. You knew him well. Why do you think he did it?"

"I don't know, Damian. Hugo's the only one who could answer that."

Lola tries Augusta several more times, but to no avail. Augusta has cut her off. Choosing to forget any attribute or sweet memory from their spent past.

She knows this isn't what she should do. Banishing such a longstanding friend. Nevertheless, Augusta feels betrayed. Humiliated. Hugo and Lola deserved each other. How could they have spawned such a lovely man?

In the coming weeks Augusta shows up unannounced to Damian's on countless occasions with offerings of baked goods, casseroles, roasts. He enjoys all these gifts, but it slowly begins to wear on him and make him feel uncomfortable. He wonders why she comes by so bloody often. After what seems the zillionth time, Damian speaks up.

"Don't get me wrong, I sure appreciate everything you do and lay at my feet, but it's getting too much. For me, anyway."

Augusta stands in the kitchen surrounded by unwashed dishes and emptied food containers.

"Alright. No problem. Still, let me tidy up this kitchen at least. It looks like a hurricane blew through here."

"No. Really, it's fine. I'll do it eventually. I've been bogged down with schoolwork. The end of term is fast around the corner and I have a multitude of deadlines. Really, I'll do it."

She quickly composes herself and stands looking at him. Examining him. As if it is the very first time she's encountered him.

"You have a lot of him in you."

"Who. What do you mean?"

"Hugo. Didn't that mother of yours ever tell you who your father was?"

"No, as a matter of fact, she hasn't."

"Well now you know."

Damian calls Lola the minute following Augusta's departure.

"Mom, was Hugo my father?"

"Yes. I mean I wasn't sure until very recently. Truthfully, just before his suicide. I'm sorry I didn't tell you."

"It's OK. I think you better come here though. Augusta seems rather crazed. She needs her friends."

Lola contacts Frankie and tells him to hop on the next flight and meet her at Augusta's. Frankie has just lost a big case and feels deflated, ready to pack it all in. He drinks too much on the flight down, contemplating his life and what it hasn't amounted to. He collects the keys to his car rental and for a second considers not getting behind the wheel; nevertheless, pulls out into the fog-filled night.

Hugo sits before the mirror in his garden studio feeling low. His nerves are dull as if all the juice from a battery has been expended. He's upset with Lola for her ongoing deception. He would have liked to have been a part of this child's life. A presence. A strength.

His drawings lay lifeless on his drafting table like death itself and his inspiration has long dried up. A fatigue has come over him that he knows he can't shake. The pills lie in his desk drawer and call to him like sirens. They cajole and nudge and whisper promises of calm and stillness. Come on. Take this slice of time. It may not come your way again. Your moment will be lost.

Irretrievable. As if a piece of fluff taken by the wind.

Row Row Row Your Boat

"The mist is heavy around me today. One can barely see beyond an arm. The wind is light and the surf is furiously pounding against the shore. It seems like all is here, and it is. As far as the things that I know. The house where I dwell, the soil that I toil. Small paths and rocky shorelines. Lichen. A clothesline and two outbuildings for the shovels, spades and rakes. Jars for the jams and Chow Chow. These are the things familiar to me, which are tactile and within sight. Things that I taste or smell or see. A ship on the horizon. Mainland to the south. A gull in the sky. Wild strawberries, blueberries and cranberries that hug the shoreline. A few black spruce and balsam. A patch of tamarack to the left... rock everywhere."

Veronica reads the letter written by her great aunt Violet. Yet she isn't sure what to do with this worn bundle of letters tied together by a faded, frayed, sky-blue ribbon. The letters arrived in an old cedar chest that had belonged to her mother Rosalie, who had recently passed, along with some journals written by Violet. She wonders why her mother had held on to these thin bits of paper that are written on onionskin stationary, which were once in the possession of her grandmother Helen. What use are they? She never knew her great aunt Violet, or her grandmother Helen for that matter. Violet disappeared long before Veronica was even a thought, or, as some say—a star in the sky.

Her great-grandfather had been the lighthouse keeper of that island. Her grandmother, Helen, had been the older of the two sisters and the family lived on the rather small island with a shoreline comprised of granite about a forty-minute boat ride from the mainland. A perilous place for any ship or sailor. This small world was all the sisters knew, notwithstanding occasional trips to dry land to see the dentist or doctor when the fevers persisted. Violet was in late adolescence when her grandmother moved to the mainland with her parents after her father fell ill and could no longer fulfill his position as keeper.

The house still stands uninhabited and beaten down from relentless Atlantic storms throughout the many years. It was once a sturdy two-storey home painted a bright white like its light-house, with white and blood red stripes visible from afar. The interior was simple, yet warm and comfy. The crew who brought the provisions enjoyed its warmth and biscuits served up by Veronica's great-grandmother who relished in the tattle of the mainland folk. "Oh, have you heard? Marian is having it on with the lobsterman's son."

Often, during high seas and fierce winds, the windows rat-tled as if the very storm could enter the house. It terrified the skins right off the sisters. There were games of Hide and Seek. Treasure island, pirates and handsome sailors that would soon res-cue them and take them away to faraway lands filled with party dresses, cupcakes. The works.

Helen married soon after arriving on the mainland, but unfortunately it was an unhappy union and she succumbed to melancholy after Rosalie's birth, dying a few years later. According to family stories trickling down through the years, Helen and Violet had been close. They had a strong affection for each other. But then how else could it have been? Two little girls living on a rock in the sea.

As Veronica reads on, it seems that Violet had dreamed of escape and at the age of fourteen had found a pen pal. She chose a local from the mainland over an exotic foreign entity to corre-spond with. Someone close. Someone who might hear her voice carry over the open sea to the windswept land.

From early childhood the girls loved island life. Once a month a supply boat arrived with provisions and books. Often toys for the girls, such as a dreamt of doll or a rocking horse, coloured pencils, crayons and chalk. They mapped out their dreams and imagined all the things they would do once they set foot on shore.

Perhaps visit a circus with elephants, where there would be a beautiful lady on a high wire wearing a sparkly costume. A strongman and clowns. Dancing dogs. They had never seen such exotic things, but had witnessed them in a photo spread in one of the city newspapers that were delivered to their father once a month. However, when he finally got to read them, the news was old. Already belonging to the past.

Occasionally special dresses came. Each one a different hue, but very much akin in style. Although there was no place to show them off, such as a birthday party with other children or on a boardwalk taking an afternoon stroll, it gave them pleasure to sport their new frocks just the same.

Their father had wanted to be a teacher and had taken several steps to achieve this goal, but the girls came early in his marriage—within nine months of each other, prompting him to get a job before completion of his studies. Consequently, he was strict in the homeschooling of his girls and made them adhere to his study curriculum of five hours per day. Often surprising them with unannounced tests on mathematics, geography, history and literature.

Playtime was restricted as more hours were allotted to their intellectual enrichment. The girls secretly resented their father for his strictness and this feeling grew, as did they, as time pushed on. Tick tock, tick tock. They constantly asked themselves, 'What's the point of all this studying if we're stuck on this friggin rock?' Violet excelled in writing and began a journal early on. Helen was less keen on her studies, preferring to play with household pets, learning to bake, collecting shells or looking for starfish which, at that time, clung in abundance to the shoreline.

Helen had kept Violet's journals along with her letters until she died, whereupon they were passed on to Rosalie from her stepmother. Rosalie didn't confide in Veronica or talk much about her mother or Violet. Helen had died when Rosalie was just three. Her father remarried and her stepmother was the one she knew, though they were never close. Her stepmother had been distant and cold like the dark Atlantic on a gloom-brimmed day.

Veronica assumed Rosalie had held on to these as a way to know her real mother. To hear Helen's voice in the words. To have an essence of whom she was, for Helen had also written many letters to Violet after she went missing at sea. Helen always mailed them back to the island, but they were always returned unopened—marked address unknown.

One early calm morning, so long ago, Violet had taken the small sloop that belonged to her father out to sea intending to meet her pen pal who had promised her a home and his heart and a place to be together away from that Godforsaken rock. That particular morning the sea was as calm as glass when she set sail for the mainland, however it turned in an instant and there came an unforgiving storm. Folk spoke about the strength of it for weeks. She never joined her sweetheart. He waited on the shoreline for hours until the hours became days.

Veronica viewed these entries as a diversion. They took her mind off her impending retirement, which she should have been jubilant about. Having finally reached this fork in the road, she only spins in circles of self-doubt and undecided destinations. Where to settle, where to drop anchor? Should she pursue the silver-haired singles scene? Solitude and death.

Veronica endured a long, boring career as a civil servant working for customs. The days had passed and melted into one another in a familiar rhythm. Occasionally there was a drug bust or some oddball with crazy sex toys hidden in his luggage, but for the most part the days mirrored each other like fog-filled mornings.

In her twenties she had travelled Europe and met a Dane. She followed him back to Denmark and lived with him in the capital for several years in complete contentment. Then, suddenly one day out of nowhere, he announced that he preferred men. This came as a shock as their sex life had been good, at least in her eyes, but obviously he had other thoughts and this was something she was unequipped to fight for.

She had loved Copenhagen and embraced all that is *hugge*. And she had been in the process of becoming a Danish citizen.

She never imagined in a thousand years that she'd head back to her provincial, uneventful past, yet she did and put on her dull, dutiful uniform day in, day out until this week. The day of her retirement.

She examines the letters her mother held onto for so long. Veronica was never close to her mother. She had wanted to be, but Rosalie was never able to bestow affection or provide guidance the way she should have. She never learned it from her stepmother.

She did feel for Veronica in the only way she knew, which was crippled by growing up in a loveless household and with a father who never got over the loss of his first wife, Helen, and her unwillingness to get on with life following the disappearance of her sister.

He took to drink after Helen's death and had a misfortunate accident after Helen's botched lobotomy. One winter eve, shortly following his marriage to his second wife, he ventured out into the cold winter night and fell off the dock across the road from the house. He slipped from the icy wood, dropped into the water and got trapped under the ice. There is a small cove that still faces all the homes in that area. The divers found his body not long after and Rosalie was left in the sole care of her stepmother.

"I hope this finds you well, my dear Colin. The weather has been miserable of late. Here it is only damp and dreary with the biting wind gnawing at every exposed and hidden section of my core. It's warm by the woodstove though. They brought us six cords of wood in the early autumn. Helen has made a ginger cake and the spicy smell lingers in the air. It's delicious too. Wish you could have some. Our cat, Sadie, is sleeping soundly next to the fire. She's a good mouser. Surprisingly, they have found their way to this island. Often, she proudly drops them at the kitchen door to await praise and a kitty treat. And we always give them to her. How are your studies going? What is your favourite subject? Our father works us hard. What are your dreams, Colin? Do you have any pets? I bet you have a dog and, if so, what is its name?"

"Violet, I was so happy to receive your letter and finally acquire a pen pal. Actually, you are my first friend by words and I'll promise to write only to you if you do the same. Let me say this. I am committing to you. To hold you in my affection and show you who I am. And yes, I have a dog. Her name is Soda Cracker. I do hope we can meet each other someday soon. If you are planning a trip to the mainland, well, perhaps I could meet you wherever you dock for the day. I have an old car that my uncle gave me. It's not much to look at, but runs fine. I could take you around and show you the sights. How does that sound? And just so you know, I'm not that keen on school. I'm going to study mechanics. I love automobiles and engines. Everything that relies on a part."

"Helen is mad at me. I think she's jealous that I've made my own faraway friend. I told her—you can make one too, but she just waved her hand and brushed me off. Stomped out into the wind and rain to take down the washing on the clothesline. I should have helped her, but I didn't."

Veronica will stop working tomorrow. She can't believe it's finally here and now that it is, it seems as if life is over instead of embarking on change. How'd it happen so fast? She remembers twenty years ago when she thought to herself, if I have all this time to go until retirement I might just kill myself. Now it is here. Then again, the end must complete itself to create the new. She looks in the mirror, contemplating plastic surgery, and imagines what her colleagues would say when they see her next. "Wow, Veronica. Retirement really agrees with you."

"Colin, now that we are starting to know one another I feel trapped here. Wouldn't it be nice to go to the cinema or take a walk? Eat ice cream—make out? Can't believe I just said that, but do you know that I think about you all the time?"

"Violet, your last letter made me blush. And believe me it ain't easy. I have three older brothers and I've heard it all. How

I would like to be near you. Smell your hair, touch your face. Touch, touch..."

Veronica has recently sold her home, having become tired of the city and all its annoyances—noise, neighbours, traffic and dirty air. She got fed up with the constant maintenance, the neverending repairs that pecked at her savings and soaked up every extra penny like a sponge. She has decided on a seaside rental and she's down for that. Ironically, the island where her relatives once lived is within eyeshot on a clear day. A thin sliver on the horizon.

She never planned on this. It is absolutely accidental, but the house conveniently presented itself and has a great sea view, lovely and unobstructed. She has dragged all of her things, including her mother's cedar chest stuffed with sentimental references that mean little to her, and will decide what to do with it all when she is settled.

The house's exterior is made of grey shingles, weathered and worn. She likes it this way, as it makes the house seem like it should be here and no other place. It has a big deck facing the sea. There are a couple of Adirondacks looking towards the water. Small boats are anchored not far from shore.

A small marina a short ways away offers sailing lessons. She always wanted to learn to sail. It has been a dream of hers since she was young. She will begin in ten days, though, unfortunately, she will be grouped with kids aged six to twelve as this is the only session in place for the summer.

"Violet, it's strange being on the mainland. All the clatter, all the people. I thought I would like it, but truly I don't. Sadie never wants to go outside anymore and sadly sits before the window staring off into space. I know she misses the island. I wish we were back there. Perhaps you're there now—just being your lazy self, not taking the time to write."

The house fits Veronica. She really likes it here with the homes spread out, not bumping against one another, but here she must be more organized with regard to shopping, as stores are a far drive away. It's a fair hop, skip and a jump to the nearest stop for food, wine or spirits.

"Violet, I miss you so. If you had any idea how much, you would never have done this. Papa is sick now from worry and Mom never stops crying. We've left the island. Papa can't fulfill his duties. The constant logs, endless notes, keeping things ship-shape and relentless repairs. I feel that you're out there somewhere. Maybe you sailed all the way to Ireland or some handsome mariner whisked you off to some enchanted land. We are in the city now. I've forwarded our new address. You have to come back to us. I've met someone."

"Colin, maybe you can visit me here. Ask a fisherman to drop you off. It would be nice if you could see how I live. I've asked Mom and Dad. They said it would be fine. You could spend some time and get to know Helen too. I'm sure you'll like her as much as me. Try to plan a trip just before a spot of bad weather. Then you'd be trapped here. Wouldn't that be swell?"

Veronica gets up early to have a balanced breakfast. She knows the open sea air will churn an appetite. She has even pre-pared a small lunch bag with a couple of sandwiches, a drink and some biscuits. She walks to the marina and spots the sign, "Welcome Sailors" and heads into the classroom. There are ten kids, each sitting around a life jacket and rope sections displaying examples of sailors' knots. The group looks at her completely perplexed when she lowers herself to the floor to join them. Veronica is fully aware that she may never be able to get up again. Her joints are stiff and locked like old rusty bolts. One boy nudges the boy next to him and they giggle. Some are spaced-out, staring at their phones. Few pay attention to the instructor.

"Colin, the last time the supply boat came, Harry, one of the crew, cornered me in the cellar. He tried to feel me up, but I pushed him off and whacked him with a bag of flour. He just grinned his toothless leer with his sour breath. Made me sick. I don't want to tell papa. He'll be so upset. Who knows? May even kill him."

"Violet, it's been so long now, yet if I stop writing to you, you will no longer exist. I can't have that. I can't cope with that notion. You will always be my sister."

After two days in the classroom, Veronica and her band of promising sailors head to the docks. There are five small sailing dinghies for the ten students. Two for each boat. The oldest student is twelve and has been matched with Veronica. His name is Will and he begrudgingly queues up next to her.

"Violet, I'm going to have a baby. If it's a girl, I'm going to call her Rosalie. I like that name, though I can't say why, but it stays in my head so I guess that's trying to tell me something. I wish I could shake this mournful hold. I should be happy about the coming child, but, truthfully, I feel like death. Why can't you be here to soothe my prickly tired mind? I'm not sure if I love my husband. What is it exactly? Am I supposed to all of a sudden feel elated that someone has swept me up and now we're hitched? Making meals, caring for a home, fulfilling my wifely duties… I'd rather be roaming the island with you. Looking for buried gems. Dreaming our lives together. Violet, do you remember the games we played? Hide and Seek. Oh how we loved that one. Perhaps you are hiding now. Doing just that. Waiting for me to find you. Come back, Violet."

"Colin, winter is fast upon us and the sea will boil and bubble and once again become its grumpy old self. It will be harder, if not impossible, for you to visit or for me to get to shore. The supply boats have more difficulties in the winter months. Sometimes it's weeks before they make it to us safely. It's a good thing that mama likes to make preserves. This week we had to kill a few chickens. Gertrude was one of them. They are like family. Gertrude liked to cuddle on my lap. I won't eat any of them. Mama roasted Gertrude this very evening. Well, I just couldn't. I was sent to my room with an empty stomach. That's why I'm writing to you now. The sky weighs heavy on us now. A fog has descended on the island for what seems to be endless nautical miles. It feels like we are the only people on earth."

"Violet, the baby came and she's a girl. I did name her Rosalie like I said I would. There's a lot of you in her, perhaps more than me. I know she will love you as much as me. Come back now. I have what you call the new mommy blues. I just can't get going. It certainly has a tight grip on me. My husband had to get help in. I just want to stay in my bed."

Veronica has settled in contentedly. She loves how the woodstove provides warmth in the cool summer evenings. She has started to go through the cedar chest and other things she dragged along in the move. She goes through the photographs and can't decide whether to cast off the ones of her former Danish love. Since him she has been single. She closed herself to new possibilities, becoming somewhat of a snob regarding the local fellas. Thinking them hicks not standing up to European charm, yet she is envious of her friends with longstanding, healthy unions with good vernacular stock.

"Violet, they've put me in the hospital. The nut house, actually. I've lost so much weight a strong breeze might blow me to you. I'll land right smack beside you in the sailboat you took. I never much cared for that boat. Didn't trust her strength. She rattled heaps and the mast wasn't as sturdy as it once was. All of her bones cried out in a strong wind and there were always mean little nips against the bow and stern. They're giving me shock treatments to try to snap me out of it. They're absolutely diabolical and don't seem to work. In the beginning he brought Rosalie to see me. Now it's been months since she has visited. I'm sure she won't recognize me anymore when I get out of here. Or should I say if? They've given no indication of my discharge date and when I ask about it, they quickly change the subject. I can't sign myself out. I'm at the mercy of my husband's wishes. He relies on the opinions of the higher powers, meaning the doctors here, and doesn't believe a single word I say. What will become of us?"

"Colin, the days are long now. How I adored this rock when I was a child. Now it feels like I can't take in a deep breath. The tightness of it all, the closeness of everyone. I'm getting weary from my lessons. I know there's so much to see out there, yet I can only see the sea and bits of vegetation and sometimes a hint of the land where you walk. I dream of wrought iron and ivy. Wild gardens filled with blooms. The lingering of a French song."

Rosalie's father had remarried shortly after the death of her mother. He had married a nurse he met at the hospital during his endless visits. And even though she had chosen a caring profession she was ungiving and difficult. An impossible read. The letters stopped following Helen's lobotomy. She never made it back to Rosalie and her husband never got over the guilt of agreeing to the procedure, taking the advice of the medical staff that it was the only viable option left.

"Colin, I've been watching the weather. Showing a keen interest in the coming weather systems that papa must chart. There seems to be a quiet time before the Nor'easter will pounce upon these waters. I'll make my departure just in the days before. I've chosen Wednesday, the day we agreed on in my last letter. I can't believe we will finally see each other. I know you already from the photograph you sent me. As you know me from mine. And look at Soda Cracker smiling for the camera too."

Veronica enjoys walking the shoreline and trails near her new rental. Her eye is always drawn far out in the blue to the island. In the past there was a fisherman who took visitors out there, but he died some time ago and since then no one has undertaken the trip. With fuel costs consistently on the rise and with so few people interested in an island visit, it lays there lonely and isolated. She conjures up what the loneliness and isolation must have felt like amongst her kin.

For the next few days Will and Veronica take their small craft out on the open water. Their instructor follows the sailors, shouting instructions and 'no no's' from a megaphone. At one point the boom that Veronica was supposed to man slipped from her grasp in high winds and her body, which doesn't respond to action as it once did, knocked poor Will into the drink. Lucky for him he was wearing a life jacket as all aspiring sailors must.

He wasn't happy about it either, but Veronica is old enough to be his grandmother and he was brought up right, so he keeps his mouth shut and says the words in his head. 'Stupid ol' bitch. Wish a shark would eat your fat ass.' Kill me now.

This morning is the last day of the course and the graduate sailors will receive their certificates shortly. But first they must complete the route mapped out for them. There is a strong breeze to fuel the sails and a sense of excitement in the air.

The students are to sail a charted passage with many ins and outs, twists and turns. All designed to test their skills. Buoys and points are accented with coloured flags. Upon completion, the students are meant to feel confident. Know the safety features of sailing and to acquire a strong appreciation for the sport itself.

Will and Veronica are in the first batch of students to undertake the exam. As they approach the second turn, the island seems to beckon her. It is as clear as any day can be and the strip of land calls to her like a siren. As if emanating from the very lighthouse itself. She makes a quick grab for the rudder, shoving Will to portside, tacking the vessel in the direction of that distant isle. She hears Will's protests, yet lets them be taken with the wind. Heading out to deep water with only the song, "Row, row, row your boat gently out to sea" echoing in her ear.

Acknowledgments

I want to thank Chris Needham and the folk at Now Or Never Publishing for believing in my third collection of short stories. I also want to thank my friend Barbara Campbell for her constant, wakeful eye. Many thanks to Jacob M. Apple, prolific New York writer, physician and playwright, to Bryan Monte, poet and editor of the *Amsterdam Quarterly*, and to Dean Serravalle, Canadian author, for their insightful blurbs. Likewise, thanks must also be extended to David Belz, editor of the *Lock Raven Review*, Maryland, and to Chris Lukather, editor of *The Writing Disorder*, Los Angeles, for theirs. And a big thanks to each and every one of you for taking the time to read my book.

Thanks to *The Writing Disorder, Lock Raven Review, Amsterdam Quarterly, Bangor Literary Review, Litbreak* and *The Los Angeles Review* for previously publishing some of the stories in this collection.

Thanks to all of you who gave encouragement along the way.